Edgar & Ellen

Fr❄ST Bites

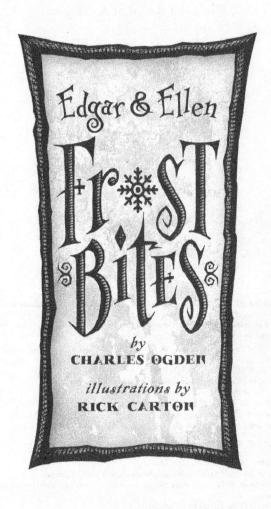

Edgar & Ellen

Fr❄ST Bites

by
CHARLES OGDEN

illustrations by
RICK CARTON

ALADDIN
New York   London   Toronto   Sydney

Watch out for Edgar & Ellen in:

Rare Beasts　　　*Edgar & Ellen*
Tourist Trap　　　*Mischief Manual*
Under Town　　　*Hair 'Em Scare 'Em*
Pet's Revenge　　*Hot Air*
High Wire
Nod's Limbs

❦ ALADDIN
An imprint of Simon & Schuster Children's Publishing Division
1230 Avenue of the Americas, New York, NY 10020
Copyright © 2008 by Star Farm Productions, LLC
All rights reserved, including the right of reproduction in whole or in part in any form.
ALADDIN and related logo are registered trademarks of Simon & Schuster, Inc.

Designed by Star Farm Productions, LLC.
The text of this book was set in Bembo, Auldroon, and Lettres Eclatees.
The illustrations in this book were rendered in pen and ink and digitally enhanced in Photoshop.
Manufactured in the United States of America
First Aladdin edition November 2008
10 9 8 7 6 5 4 3 2 1
Library of Congress Control Number 2007046411
ISBN-13: 978-1-4169-5464-4
ISBN-10: 1-4169-5464-3

HERE IS MY DEDICATION—

To valiant *Val*, *Marie*, and *Mo*,
For drawing back the archer's bow;
Diane and *Tom*, like *William Tell*,
Hit the target, true and well.

—CHARLES

Follow Trails Gone Cold...

Prologue

A frigid whorl of air blew fat flakes of snow up Ellen's right nostril—her left was frozen shut. She would have grimaced, but her face was too numb to move.

"Edgar, g-get that f-fire going," she said through chattering teeth.

Her twin brother rubbed together two wicker reeds, hoping to set fire to the rest of the hot-air balloon basket heaped in the snowdrift.

They had traveled in the airship for weeks, leaving behind the warmth and familiarity of Nod's Limbs and trading it, day by day, for air that bit ever more crisply into their skin, and fields below that changed from green to brown to (as of three days ago) white. The weather turned cruel, and the balloon itself had become laden with sheets of ice during an arctic blizzard. With fuel for the burner and rocket thrusters running out, the basket had sunk lower and lower, until it scraped the rocky ground. They could see nothing beyond the dense curtain of snowflakes, and when the balloon itself brushed a rocky outcropping, it cracked apart like peanut brittle. Now there was nothing left in Edgar and Ellen's world but freezing winds, snow, and a pile of wicker that refused to catch fire.

"I s-saw a spark!" called Edgar. "White hot sp-sparks . . . everywhere . . ."

"For the l-last time, those are *sn-sn-snowflakes*," croaked Ellen.

"Right you are," said Edgar deliriously. "Burning h-hot snowflakes . . . Come here, l-little fellas. . . ."

He began to dance about, attempting to hug the snowflakes for warmth.

Ellen pulled a holey blanket over her head, the only real protection she had against the weather besides the ratty footie pajamas she and her brother always wore. In just a few hours of snowy torment on the forsaken mountainside, her brother had gone mad, truly mad, and she knew she could not be far behind. She glanced at Pet for some sign of hope, but the little creature had drawn its mound of hair around its single eye, until it appeared to be no more than a fuzzy snowball. Whether it was warm under that insulation she could not say, for Pet had stopped moving an hour ago, and the blowing snow was beginning to pile up around it. Soon it would be buried and lost. As would they all.

Her brother pulled his arms all the way inside his pajamas, leaving the sleeves to flap maniacally as he bounded in circles, singing nursery rhymes. Ellen's lids narrowed, and she could feel ice working to seal them shut. Would her eyes close now for the final time?

Then she heard Death itself call to her.

"Four," came a ghostly voice on the wind.

"M-Minutes?" she asked the swirling snow. "Or hours?"

"What did you say, Sister?" said Edgar, stopping his frolic.

"D-D-Death calls, Brother," Ellen moaned. "Proclaiming the m-m-moment of our d-doom. In *f-four.*"

"Sister, you've gone mad," Edgar announced. "Stark-raving, full-tilt, nuts-to-you—"

That's when the golf ball hit Edgar in the head and knocked him out cold.

The little ball rolled to a stop near Ellen's toes. It really did look like a golf ball, down to the pitted dimples across its surface, except this ball was neon purple and stood out brilliantly against the snow.

A man's head popped up from behind a rock. His bushy beard was crusted with ice, and he wore a Scottish tam o' shanter (though the thin, little hat did not look like it could possibly keep him very warm).

"There you are, little rascal!" the man said. He called back over his shoulder, "Found it, Knute! Going to be a two-stroke penalty to get you out of the rough, you betcha."

Another head popped up beside the first. This one wore a sensibly warm woolen hat, but when this fellow leaped over the rock to stand before her, Ellen noticed that he had on insanely ugly golfing knickers.

"Ah, *snorft*!" he cursed. He pointed a golf club at the purple ball. "I can play it where it lies, you watch. Little girl, would you mind moving your toes? Torbald here thinks I can't get back on the fairway with a five iron."

"Pff," said Torbald. "Ten *frøstendollers* says you slice it left."

Ellen considered her situation before responding. "Are you Death?"

"No, I'm Knute," said the man. "I have a cousin Dethborg, but you probably don't know him. He lives in Hjarnbladder."

"Oh," said Ellen. "I see. You h-hit my brother with your ball, Knute."

"Well, I *did* call *fore*," said Knute. "Oh, but maybe you didn't hear me over the howling winds. I'm sure sorry about that. You should head back to town and have his noggin looked at."

"T-T-T-T— Did you say t-t-t-t—"

"You can take our golf cart," said Knute.

Ellen peeked over the rock and saw their "cart": a small red dogsled attached to a team of huskies. The dogs also wore plaid tams. "I believe I'll accept your offer," she said at last.

"Good!" said Knute. "The dogs know the way to Frøsthaven Happy Healing Hospital, don't you, pups?" One of the huskies yipped. "We've got a couple of fur parkas for you too. Looks like you caught a bit of a chill, eh?"

"Hurry up there, Knute," said Torbald. "There's

nine holes to go before it gets cold."

Knute sighed. "Wish it weren't so *skortkraggen* hard to get a tee time on this course."

With that, Knute sliced the ball wide left. It ricocheted off a jagged finger of ice and plummeted into a crevasse, never to be seen again.

1. Frøsthaven

The town of Frøsthaven was the most pleasant place on Earth—or so one might think, had one not grown up in Nod's Limbs. It boasted charming shopping districts ("The World's Most Whopping Shopping") and scintillating historic monuments ("Ern 'Bearclaw' Nortsk grappled three polar bears on this spot in 1888 without spilling his coffee").

Any of a hundred other charms would have earned Frøsthaven a beloved spot in its citizens' hearts, but without a doubt each man, woman, and child were proudest of their town's ice sculptures. In most places, an ice sculpture entailed an artist chiseling a frozen block into teddy bears or flying geese—lovely, to be sure, but mere peanuts to the citizens of Frøsthaven. In this town, ice sculptures were more than art, they were the very building blocks of the community. Every house, every office, every shop, restaurant, library, and school—every structure right down to the outhouses—were chunks of ice that had been lovingly whittled into swirling, swooping, poetic shapes.

The twins, now bundled in borrowed furs, could see this gleaming vision as they rode over a ridge on the speeding golf sled (well, Edgar would have seen it, had he not still been unconscious). The storm had broken just as they crested the lip of a vast valley, and a bejeweled town spread out before them like a model railroad village. It seemed as if a half-mad glassblower had picked up his tools in the middle of a fever dream and conjured himself the largest glass menagerie the world had ever seen. Spires of ice caught the now-piercing sunlight and refracted it into dancing rainbows. And it wasn't just the spires—every cupola, steeple, gazebo, garden shed, weather vane, clock tower, and, yes, covered bridge scattered glimmering light over this snow-lined valley as if a vat of glitter had exploded in the center of the city.

As the dogs pulled the sled through this winter wonderland, Ellen reflected on all that had happened in the past weeks, and what had led them on an adventure they never could have guessed they'd take.

It was all Stephanie Knightleigh's fault, of course, as if that were any surprise. She had gotten her hands on a significant amount of balm from the collapsed spring in Nod's Limbs, a mysterious substance that had at least one remarkable quality: If consumed, it could keep a person alive indefinitely. It was also highly explosive, and Pet's only form of food. The twins had been happy to leave it at that, but then Stephanie had returned and stolen valuable notes and equipment from their cohort, Augustus Nod, and here they were: chasing down the redheaded princess to stop her from doing, well, whatever it was she planned to do.

Ellen had to admit they'd not been very well-informed when they'd begun their journey—they weren't even positive Stephanie had come this way—but they did know that anyone so obsessed with balm was a danger, possibly on a global scale. Mad Duke Disease, a form of megalomania brought on by too much consumption of the balm, had led to more than one full-scale war in the past.

And then there was the Heimertz family, a traveling circus that protected balm springs around the world. They had vanished, and Ronan Heimertz, the twins' loyal groundskeeper, had left to find them, and had likewise disappeared. Nod and Heimertz's wife, Madame Dahlia, had set off after him, and the twins after Stephanie, in a race to discover the meaning behind these strange events. And what had they to show for it?

"Hypothermia," mumbled Ellen. Edgar stirred next to her and raised his head, gazing out at the dazzling scenery.

"So sparkly," he muttered. "Is it spun sugar? Am I in dessert heaven? Where all good desserts go when they die?"

Ellen grabbed the frozen Pet-ball from her brother's lap and hit him with it.

"Snap out of it," she said. "This isn't Death—but it may actually be worse."

She pointed at a wooden sign standing at the side of the ice road:

WELCOME TO FRØSTHAVEN!
THE CHARMINGEST LITTLE TOWN
IN THE ARCTIC CIRCLE

In the corner of the sign, a doe-eyed snowball wearing a top hat waved at them; above him a word balloon read: "Come on in! You'll have a (snow) ball!"

"Charmingest?" said Ellen.

Edgar glanced around. "Um, why are we in a dogsled?"

"Oh, you're going to love this story," said Ellen.

As Ellen filled him in, the huskies pulled them deeper into the valley. To the north of town, a behemoth of a mountain lorded over Frøsthaven. The monstrosity seemed out of place, alone in the center of the valley, as if it had been cast away by the distant mountain ranges for being too big. And the twins noticed another curious thing: Between the town and the mountain rose a high, glittering wall made entirely of ice, built as if to repel an army of invading Vikings.

At last they drew closer to town, and signs of activity increased, all of it as normal as one might expect: bundled children skipping home from school, mail carriers delivering letters and packages, crossing guards assisting pedestrians across streets.

But so, too, did these familiar scenes feel distinctly *off*. An old woman on a park bench fed breadcrumbs not to a flock of pigeons, but penguins; the clumsy birds nudged one another out of the way for mouthfuls of stale crust. A man on a ladder hoisted a bucket and paintbrush up the side of his house, but instead of spreading a garish yellow or green paint, as he might have in Nod's Limbs, he brushed on a coat of water, which froze instantly and reinforced the ice exterior. And whereas Nod's Limbsian homeowners like Mr. Poshi trimmed their topiary hedges into unicorns and cocker spaniels, the gardeners of Frøsthaven sculpted the snow in their front yards into the shapes of bushes and trees and perfectly straight hedgerows.

The twins sailed past a frozen pond, upon which stood bleachers full of fans in blue and pink parkas. The fans cheered athletes who swung baseball-like bats at snowballs and skated from base to base.

"Yes, fans, it's a lovely day for some *basbøll*," chirped an announcer. "Now put your mittens together for your Frøsthaven Joostentaglers!"

"I didn't know there were towns up here," said Edgar.

"We don't even know where *here* is," said Ellen.

"Thanks to that sketchy map—and your totally nonexistent navigational skills—we could be hundreds of miles from the Black Diamond Glacier."

"I'm an excellent navigator!" said Edgar. "You're the one who threw the compass over the side—"

"I *dropped* it because you cranked the thrusters too hard," said Ellen. "We lost the last of our food the same way, or don't you remember?"

"Well, we were almost *out* of food, so big deal," said Edgar. He slumped back down onto the sled and patted Pet, which was slowly unfurling from its curled-up state. "Do you think Stephanie passed through here?"

"I don't hear any high-pitched complaining, so maybe not," said Ellen. "But if so, we'll find her."

"I wonder what's so special about the Black Diamond Glacier," Edgar muttered for probably the eight-hundredth time since they'd started their journey. "Stephanie already has a bucket of Nod's balm—she could live forever if she wanted to. What else does she hope to do with it?"

"I'm looking forward to stomping the answers out of her," said Ellen. "And, you know, saving humanity and all."

"*Saving humanity,*" repeated Edgar. "Do you really

think Nod meant that, or was he just exaggerating? After all, this is just one annoying small-town princess we're talking about."

Ellen grunted. She looked around at the sparkling town.

"Like living under a disco ball," she grumbled, and as she urged the dogs deeper into the valley, the twins sang:

> *Just when we thought one would suffice,*
> *We've found a Nod's Limbs trapped in ice,*
> *A colder twist on nicey-nice,*
> *This bland, snowflaky paradise.*
> *Across the frozen fields we've trolled*
> *All in the hopes of catching hold*
> *Of more than just the common cold:*
> *To see our rival's plots unfold.*
> *Now at the far side of the Earth,*
> *We'll see what twintuition's worth.*

2. Day Day Fest

The dogs pulled them down a wide boulevard toward the heart of town. Hardy trees in enormous planters lined the sides of the road; Ellen recognized birchbite pines, chill-backed aspens, tundra spruce, and some unknown variations of boreal tamaracks, all resilient, brutish species, but pruned here into perfect cones and pear shapes.

Traffic increased on the road—not cars, but more dogsleds, as well as sleighs pulled by reindeer, elk, and in one case, a team of walruses. The people on these conveyances could be heard humming or whistling, and when they passed one another they burst into carols sung in four-part harmony. These happy masses drove toward the center of the city, sweeping the twins' dogsled along with them. Edgar and Ellen could see the town square ahead of them, an open space filled with colorful flags, streamers, and banners proclaiming some kind of festival. A bell tower rose over the square, much taller than the clock tower of Nod's Limbs, and just as stately. Many festivalgoers in jaunty hats and lederhosen danced roundelays and waved cheerily to one another.

"I'm having a déjà vu experience," said Edgar.

"No kidding," said Ellen, as they rode by a stage and banner above it, reading:

HAPPY DAY DAY, EVERYONE!
IT'S AN ICE DAY TO CELEBRATE DAY!

"I don't even know what that means," said Edgar.

"This could be a Nod's Limbs celebration," said Ellen. "Remember the 'Hooray for Cheering' festival?"

Edgar shuddered.

A two-hundred piece marching band, complete with two full rows of shiny silver sousaphones, rounded the corner playing a thunderous march. The neat rows of musicians were high-stepping straight toward the sled, and the twins braced for impact. But every marcher in the band—every piccolo, trombone, B-flat cornet, and flügelhorn—stepped neatly out of the way as they passed the sled, tipping their plume-topped hats without miss-

ing a beat. A bass drum player even waved and said, "Have a super day!"

"Okay, this is just eerie," said Ellen. "It's like Nod's Limbs on ice."

Edgar stroked his chin. "I wonder . . ."

The dogs took a left off the town square and slowed to a stop in front of a crystal clear hospital. The frozen walls were made of water so pure, the twins could plainly see doctors and nurses going about their rounds, and patients lying in beds watching TV.

"Do we really need to get your head checked?" asked Ellen as they got off the sled.

Edgar rapped his skull. "Sister, it's as sharp as ever."

"*Lumpy* as ever, maybe," said Ellen. "So now what?"

"As long as everyone is distracted by a festival, we could infiltrate some kind of information office, maybe Town Hall, to find out more about this place," said Edgar. He opened his satchel. "If the locks are made of ice too, I may need some practice picking one—"

"Always making things as complicated as possible," said Ellen. "Hey, Nurse Snowpants!" she called to an approaching woman in a sea foam green snowsuit that, if it hadn't been puffed fat with down, would have looked like hospital scrubs. "We just arrived in town and could use some help."

The woman smiled at once. "Oh! Out-of-towners! Anything you need, just ask—Frøsthaven takes extra care of its tourists, no matter what you've heard!"

"Er, okay," said Ellen. "For starters, what *is* this place?"

"Frøsthaven, of course," said the woman. "The Charmingest Little—"

"Yeah, we know," said Ellen. "But we're looking specifically for the Black Diamond Glacier. Ever heard of it?"

"Heard of it? Why, you're *on* it," said the woman brightly.

"I knew it!" said Edgar.

"The Black Diamond Glacier is a wide sheet of solid ice twenty-two *crickles* long and seven wide, lying just above the dormant volcano," said the woman, sounding well-rehearsed. "Frøsthaven is situated at the midpoint, in the shadow of Snorgpeke Mountain. Not even Hognorsk and Ødansk offer as many family-friendly winter activities as Frøsthaven, where we have the best skiing, sledding, and *otter-*

horken. Oh, and you're in time for blubber-rendering season! Fresh *derflootle* is the most wonderful thing on Earth!"

"Mmm, super," said Ellen as the nurse resumed her walk. "Can't wait."

Edgar cracked his knuckles. "Ha! My excellent navigational skills have taken us right to the spot!"

"This spot is only the center of inanity," said Ellen.

"Quiet, Sister, I'm having a thought."

"Nod help us."

"No, listen. You said it yourself—it's like we never left Nod's Limbs. This festival. These *people*. Each one of them is happier and doofier than the next."

"So?" said Ellen.

"Topiary snow hedges? The happy tour-guide act? *Charmingest?* These people are zombies of niceness, same as any Nod's Limbsian!"

"And again I say, so? Apparently we're just unlucky enough to have found the *two* most sickeningly sweet places on Earth."

"What if it's not coincidence?" said Edgar. "Just hear me out. Balm does funny things to people in diluted form—remember how Nod used it in candle wax, and the burning candles made people feel 'wholesome'?"

"Yes."

"So what if balm is the common thread between Nod's Limbs and Frøsthaven? What if living near a balm spring affects the people themselves?"

"You mean like it seeps into the water supply?" Ellen tugged a pigtail thoughtfully.

"Something like that," said Edgar. "I bet you anything there's an actual spring somewhere nearby. And if so, then Stephanie must be too. That could even be the reason why she's here."

"Well, we drank Nod's Limbs water, and we're no one's zombie," said Ellen.

Edgar's face fell. "Good point. I wish I could get my hands on Nod's laboratory equipment. This bears further experimentation. . . ."

"Don't get distracted," said Ellen. "We have to *find* Stephanie first."

"Yes, yes, Stephanie, too," said Edgar, pacing back and forth. "Why wouldn't *she* have been affected after all those years? She doesn't have a nice bone in her body. . . ."

A rumbling sound echoed down the street, breaking Edgar's ramblings.

"What's that?" asked Ellen.

A moment later a penguin rounded the corner, half waddling, half sliding on its belly, as fast as it could go. It was followed by another, then another, then a whole horde of racing penguins. Behind them, a crowd of people surged around the corner, chasing after the black-and-white birds, whooping and hollering as they ran. Even after living in Nod's Limbs for their whole lives, it was the strangest thing Edgar and Ellen had ever seen.

But they did not have time to ponder the spectacle, for the mass of penguins and people was coming right for them, taking up the entire street. The twins and Pet were forced to turn and flee, and were soon caught up in the racing crowd and swept along for the ride.

3. Penguin's Run

"What's going on?" shouted Ellen to Edgar, who could only shrug back. But a helpful lad running next to them answered her question.

"It's the annual Running of the Penguins," he yelled back to Ellen over the din of the crowd. "Frøsthaven tradition!"

"I thought penguins only lived in Antarctica," Edgar said.

"Not the *Skroog* species!" the boy replied. "They're migratory!"

"Okay, this place is officially *more* ridiculous than Nod's Limbs," Ellen muttered.

By now the runners had reached the town square, where they herded the birds into a large pen. Edgar and Ellen collapsed against each other, panting, but the boy they'd met was barely out of breath. He looked a few years older than the twins, tall, with big shoulders and white-blond hair. He stuck out an enormous hand.

"My name's Gürlf. New to Frøsthaven, are you?"

"Just . . . visiting . . ." Ellen gasped, shaking his hand and wincing at his strength.

"Excellent!" exclaimed Gürlf. "You came at the best time! The Day Day Festival marks the day that's day all day long!"

"Huh?" said Edgar.

"We're so close to the pole, during parts of the year the sun doesn't set at all. There's no night, only day."

"There goes sneaking around in the dark, then," said Ellen.

"That's why we fit as much as possible into one

23

day," Gürlf continued. "There's the ice-cake brunch, then the Running of the Penguins, then the *derflootle*-eating contest, and of course the Icey 500, the premier sleigh race of the North."

"Of course," said Edgar.

"Listen, Gruff, it's been really nice chatting, but my brother and I need to be going—" Ellen tried to extricate her hand from Gürlf's strong paw.

"You're hungry, aren't you?" he said. "Looks like you haven't eaten in weeks! Well, a *derflootle*-eating contest will fix that. And are you in for a treat! It's—"

"Blubber-rendering season. We heard," said Ellen. "Lucky us."

Gürlf grabbed Edgar with his other hand and pulled the twins along through the teeming crowd toward a tent at the far end. Pet snuck along behind them, trying to avoid the stomping snow boots.

A group of men ran about the penguin pen, trying to round up the birds.

"Penguin wranglers," Gürlf explained. "They'll release them back into the wild."

He dragged the twins through the tent flap. It was filled with people sitting at rows of long tables. At one end chefs moved around huge steaming vats, spooning heaps of meaty blubber blobs onto plates. Servers scurried back and forth, delivering the plates to the tables.

"Uncle! I got two extra!" Gürlf called up the center row, and he dragged the twins down the aisle. A man in a silver tracksuit with goggles strapped to his bald head waved a hand bigger than Gürlf's.

"Newcomers! Brilliant!" he exclaimed in a deep, throaty voice. "Move down, move down," he said to the man and woman who sat on either side of him. "Make way for our guests!"

Gürlf deposited Edgar and Ellen on either side of the man, clapping each of them on the shoulder. The gesture nearly knocked them over.

"Ah, yes, you must be the tourists—Knute told me you looked sickly, but I had no idea that golf ball did such damage. Well, nothing a *gnorm*'s worth of *derflootle* won't fix! But where are my manners? I'm Mayor Wiig Kerschloggendöcke. If that's too much of a mouthful, just call me Big Wiigie. I just want you to know, it is Frøsthaven policy to take the most super-special care of our out-of-towners!"

"So we hear," said Edgar. "And while we, uh, appreciate the invitation to participate—"

But he was cut off by Big Wiigie, who throttled

the twins in two jolly underarm hugs. Gürlf sat down across the table from them.

"So how have you enjoyed Frøsthaven so far?" asked Big Wiigie.

"It's been . . . interesting," said Edgar.

"I'll bet!" said Big Wiigie. "There's no place like it in the world!"

The twins exchanged glances.

"That's right," said a woman who deposited a plate of steaming *derflootle* in front of Ellen. Her nametag said AUD. "We have all sorts of interesting festivals and parades and celebrations, all year round. Why, I've seen more amazing things in Frøsthaven than anywhere else. Sure, I've never been anywhere else, but when you see a man dissect a butterfly, sew it back together, then have that same butterfly *fly away again*, good as new, well, I can't believe you can top it. Even if you go all the way to Timbuktu!".

Ellen choked, and Big Wiigie slapped her on the back.

"Careful there, missy. You haven't even tasted the *derflootle* yet!"

"What did you say? About the man who dissected the butterfly?" Ellen asked Aud.

"Gave me the *bumbergoosens*, it did," said Aud.

"The whole circus did, mind you. Dancing peacocks and mime police. They're an odd bunch, those Heimertzes, but their acts are wonderful. Ack! Peder! You're *skrrorten* the *derflootle!*" And Aud hurried off to tend to the kitchen emergency.

"The Heimertz Circus was here?" Edgar asked, his eyes shining with hope.

"Six months back or so," said Big Wiigie. "It's a shame you missed it, if you like that kind of thing."

"Where did the circus set up camp?" asked Edgar. "It doesn't seem like there'd be enough room in town."

"They always set up the big top in Mudjut Meadow," said Gürlf. "It's just beyond the wall, between here and Snorgpeke Mountain."

"Excellent," said Ellen. "Then that's where we want to go."

Gürlf and Big Wiigie glanced worriedly at each other.

"Oh, you don't want to go there," Big Wiigie assured them. "Nothing to do, for one, not when there's no circus. Just snow and ice and tundra moles. Very boring."

"We're naturalist students," said Ellen. "We came specifically to see the tundra moles."

"Oh dear, oh dear," murmured Big Wiigie. "We don't like people unfamiliar with the area to go wandering around out there. Especially not after what happened to that sweet little red-haired girl from Nod's Limbs."

4. Ellen Takes a Bet

The twins' eyes bulged.

"Did you say 'red-haired girl from Nod's Limbs?'" asked Ellen. "Where did she go?"

"No one knows," said Gürlf. "She was staying in the Two Seasons Hotel just off the square. And one morning she left with a bunch of hiking equipment and never came back."

"*Hoo gar!* Have we ever got some hot *derflootle* here!" Big Wiigie exclaimed, shooting Gürlf a stern look.

"We want to go exactly where the red-haired girl went," said Ellen. "She's a . . . a rival of ours. If she collects more mole specimens than we do, we'll flunk."

Again Big Wiigie and Gürlf exchanged worried glances.

"Tell you what," said Gürlf. "If you can eat more *derflootle* than me, I'll take you out there myself. If not, I'll take you around town tomorrow instead. Deal?"

Ellen looked doubtfully at the fleshy meat on her plate. It had a weird smell, like mayonnaise left too long in the sun. She had a feeling it wouldn't taste any better.

Gürlf was tying a plastic bib around his neck. He smiled appreciatively at his meal and licked his lips.

"You're on," said Ellen.

By now the entire tent had been served, and everyone participating in the contest had piles of *derflootle* in front of them. Aud stood at the front of the tent next to a dinner bell.

"On your mark," she called out, "get set, *GORM*!" And she clanged the bell.

Ellen took this to mean "Go," so she set into her food. She picked up a blob of meat and shoved it in her mouth, barely chewing before gulping it down. It wasn't as bad as she'd expected, actually. It was a little bitter, but tender, and low on gristle.

Gürlf was already halfway done with his plate, and Ellen knew she had to pick up the pace. She started slurping up two or three pieces at a time,

and found that the blobs slid straight down her throat without chewing. It was a weird sensation, but it seemed to be working: she was gaining on the competition.

Gürlf finished his plate, and a second later a server had switched it out with a full one. Soon after that someone did the same for Ellen. She barely looked up before diving into her second batch.

By the third plate she was tooth and tooth with Gürlf, but she could feel her stomach making unnatural noises. She thought she could vaguely hear Edgar cheering her on, but all her focus was centered on the plate in front of her. At the other tables, most people had given up, but now Ellen and Gürlf were on their fourth plates.

Gürlf moaned as he swallowed. He was slowing down, but so was Ellen. She had just three pieces of meat left before her fifth plate. Her stomach felt as if she'd drunk cement. Two pieces. One piece.

She looked up at Gürlf, who was also about to eat the last bit on his plate. He held it in his hand, staring at it woozily. The *derflootle* had clearly taken as big a toll on him as it had on Ellen. With a trembling hand he put the meat to his mouth, but just as he was about to shove it in, he fell forward onto the table in a dead faint. The meat splatted on the floor.

The gathered crowd looked at Ellen, but no one made a sound. She closed her eyes, compressed the meat into a ball, and crammed it into her mouth. She chewed for a moment, swallowed, and promptly passed out.

5. Red Hairing

Ellen woke on a wonderfully soft mattress, covered in blankets. She had forgotten it was possible to be so comfortable, and for a moment she thought she was back home in Nod's mansion in Nod's Limbs. Then she burped, and the smell of *derflootle* brought her back to the present.

She rubbed her eyes and sat up. The room was dimly lit, with heavy curtains shielding the windows, but what was remarkable was that the floor, ceiling, and walls were all made of ice. Ellen felt the wall behind her; it was freezing cold and wet, but frosted so that she couldn't see into the room beyond.

The door flew open and Edgar burst in, carrying Pet and his satchel.

"Good, you're up. We've got things to do," he said.

"What time is it?" asked Ellen. Her stomach burbled angrily.

"Early. Sixish, I'd say. But no one goes to sleep around here on Day Day, apparently. Unless they've eaten four plates of *derflootle*, that is."

Edgar strode to the window and tied back the

curtains. The brightest sunlight Ellen had ever seen flooded the room, sparkling on the ice interior.

"What happened?" she asked, shading her eyes as they adjusted to the brilliance.

"You should have seen yourself. A right pig, you were, gulping that stuff down. It was really impressive, Sister. And you beat Gürlf! Big, hulking, three-times-your-size Gürlf. Which means he has to take us out to Mudjut Meadow or wherever Stephanie went. He's meeting us here at eight, so we've only got a couple hours."

"A couple hours to do what?"

"To snoop! Big Wiigie was so embarrassed that his nephew challenged you into a food coma that he put us up at the Two Seasons—the same hotel Stephanie stayed in. I've done some reconnaissance and found out which room was hers. We don't have long to search it for clues."

Clutching her swollen and occasionally quivering stomach, Ellen followed Edgar and Pet up two flights of stairs (made of ice, of course, and slippery) to the Viking King Penthouse Suite.

"This is it," said Edgar. "The bellhop said Stephanie left with a great big backpack filled with stuff, but hopefully there's something here that can help us."

"Stephanie carried her own luggage? I might die of shock," said Ellen.

Edgar could see the tumblers in the ice lock on the door, and he was sure he could crack the lock in no time. It proved far more difficult than he imagined, however, since a lock made entirely of ice did not have the same sturdy feel beneath his fingertips as, say, a Safemaster Supreme padlock or a Mortal Coil–brand dead bolt or one of a hundred other locks he had defeated in Nod's Limbs.

Finally Ellen shoved him aside and blew her hot *derflootle* breath into the lock until it melted, then she pushed the door open with a finger.

"Ridiculous town," she muttered as they entered the room.

As in Ellen's room, light illuminated the icy chamber. It was fairly empty, though it looked like housekeeping had not yet been in to clean it. A quick survey of the writing desk showed that it was covered with crusty white goop that looked very much like dried balm. Pet confirmed this by sweeping over the desk, absorbing what it could of the substance. It nodded at the twins, sated by the meager snack.

"Look at this," said Ellen, examining the wall

next to the desk. Stephanie had used the ice wall as a kind of chalkboard, writing various notes and symbols on it with a marker. None of it made any sense to the twins, but much of it reminded them of similar markings they'd seen in Nod's journals— all except the places where Stephanie had been practicing her signature with increasing levels of flourish, and a group of doodles showing a stick-figure Stephanie feeding two striped stick figures to a lopsided alligator.

"Yep, she's gone mad," said Ellen.

"NL + BD + LL + CF + something I can't make

out," Edgar read off the wall. "Seems like Steph's been conducting her own experiments on the balm. If there's another spring nearby, that's probably what she set off to find."

"She was nuts for power before she ever came in contact with this stuff," said Ellen. "I can't imagine how she'll be now that's she's gone and given herself Mad Duke Disease."

"But what's she doing with it?" Edgar asked. "What's the big threat?"

"Don't you think a Stephanie who lives forever is threat enough?" asked Ellen.

"Let's just hope we can find her," said Edgar.

5. The Ice Wall

An hour later, the twins and Pet were waiting in the Two Seasons' ice lobby when Gürlf strode in, his cheeks ruddy from the cold.

"What a race!" he cried, rubbing his hands together. "Sorry you had to miss it, er, Ellen." He smiled abashedly at Ellen, and the twins thought they could hear his stomach rumble. "That was quite a showing you gave at the contest yesterday. Congratulations. The best girl won."

"And that means you have to take us to Mudjut Meadow," said Ellen. "A deal's a deal."

"That's why I'm here," said Gürlf. "But are you sure you wouldn't rather tour Frøsthaven instead? The Joostentaglers play again today for the regional championship!" The twins just shook their heads, and Gürlf nodded glumly. "Follow me, then."

The twins and Pet followed Gürlf out into the cold air and crossed through the square toward the great wall of ice. They passed a group of people gathered around a magnificent sledge of ice strapped to two hulking reindeer. The crowd clapped and cheered, and in the center, Knute was bowing and waving. He wore a wreath of holly branches around his neck and held up a silver cup. He called out when he saw the twins.

"Hi there, kiddos! Come to congratulate me on my big win?"

"You won the Icey 500?" asked Edgar.

"Me and old Bëtsye here," said Knute, his eyes twinkling. "My specially modified ice dredge. Fastest in the valley!"

The twins, Pet, and Gürlf continued on their way through town, past cheery dog walkers, fence-gossiping neighbors, dads polishing their dogsleds, and children hawking frozen lemonade from home-made stands, ever nearing the ice wall.

"What's with the wall, anyway?" Edgar asked Gürlf.

"It's just, er, protection," said Gürlf. "From the high winds. And the . . . mountain."

"The mountain?" asked Ellen. "What's wrong with the mountain?"

Gürlf didn't say anything for a moment. He looked out at Snorgpeke in the distance, beyond the wall, then back at the twins.

"I'm only telling you this because you're so bent on leaving the safety of the city," he said. "But just beyond Mudjut Meadow is the Glöggenheim, and that is not a place you want to be."

"Why not?" asked Ellen.

"It's the wrong side of the reindeer tracks, that's why," said Gürlf. "It's dark and scraggly, and anyone who goes up there doesn't come back."

"What's up there?" asked Edgar. "Is it the mouth of the volcano?"

"No, that's been dormant for years. It's the Glögg."

"The what?"

Gürlf hesitated again. "Big Wiigie would freeze

my fingers if he knew I was telling you this," he said, and sighed. "The Glögg lives on the Glöggenheim, and those that go up that *skortkraggen* slope never come back. The Glögg gets them."

"Yes, yes, but what is a Glögg?" Ellen asked impatiently.

"Not something you ever want to meet," said Gürlf, "and that's why no one's to go out to Mudjut Meadow on their own. We tried to stop your redhaired friend, but she wouldn't listen."

The stream of dog-sledding commuters had thinned and the houses had grown farther apart as they neared the edge of town. Edgar and Ellen pestered Gürlf for more answers, but the usually loquacious lad refused to say another word on the subject of Glöggs. Then, through a break in the snow hedges, they came upon it: the massive wall of ice.

It was at least thirty feet tall, a solid frosty blue mass. The smooth sides seemed impossible to scale, and lookout posts were interspersed along its top. The only way through was a short, narrow iron gate at the base of one of these lookouts, concealed from the outside by more snow hedges. From the inside it was barred by a long steel pole.

"What are we waiting for?" said Edgar. "Let's go."

After one more pleading look at the twins, Gürlf reluctantly removed the bar, and they all trudged through the gate.

Mudjut Meadow bore none of the usual hallmarks of something so named: There were no butterflies flitting from wildflower to wildflower, no sun-dappled brook babbling through a thicket of lilacs, no children skipping merrily through lush grass. Instead, this meadow was a barren expanse of whiteness, exactly as Big Wiigie had described. At the far edge, Snorgpeke Mountain rose abruptly out of the earth. Mountains, as a general rule, are stately and majestic giants, towering over their surroundings like Greek Titans proclaiming their dominion over all they survey. To Edgar and Ellen, Snorgpeke seemed more than a mere Titan—it was Zeus himself, telling the Titans to shove over. The mountain was broad and burly and covered by a peaceful blanket of snow. Peaceful but for the western slope, that is; this foreboding expanse of gnarled rock was full of craggy precipices and crevasses marring the face of the mountain. Where the other slopes raced daringly toward the heavens, this one merely slouched along, wrinkling itself into shadowy folds as if it had something to hide.

"Is that the Glöggenheim?" asked Edgar, pulling a vial from his satchel.

"Aye," said Gürlf. "And this is as close as you'd ever want to get to it. Some places on this Earth are just bad to their roots. You can feel it." He shuddered. "But that's not why we're here. Now, if you want to find the best tundra moles, you have to—"

He couldn't finish, because Edgar had blown the contents of the vial into Gürlf's face. Gürlf broke out in a coughing fit, dropping to the ground.

"Coughing Pepper," said Edgar to Ellen. "Remember? I borrowed it from Eugenia back in Nod's Limbs."

He turned to the wheezing Gürlf. "Sorry, Gürlf, we really appreciate all your help, but we've got to leave you here. It's for your own good, of course. Now chew some snow; you'll be all right soon. But we'll be long gone."

And with that, Edgar, Ellen, and Pet hurried off across the meadow. Gürlf, doubled over behind them, tried to call out.

"But—*cogg*—where—*grawk*—are—*cack*—you—*horck*—going?" he gasped. "Didn't you hear—*garg*—what I told you?"

But his pleas were lost to the wind, which swept

more swiftly here than in town. The sun had dipped behind some clouds, and the twins shivered to their bones. They made for a forest of pines at the foot of the Glöggenheim. The trees blocked some of the cold gales, but something about the battered, wind-whipped pines seemed to cast a gray pall over them, giving them an inexplicable shudder of loneliness. To combat the feeling the twins sang quietly:

> *The cold, it pierces these fur hides,*
> *But colder still, the dread inside,*
> *At what foul creature yon resides*
> *Across the snowy rime.*
> *What secrets does this mountain keep*
> *Lost inside its rocky deep?*
> *What shall we find when up the steep*
> *And craggy slope we climb?*

7. The Mountain Comes Down

At the edge of the tree line, the great gray menace of the Glöggenheim lay before them, warning them not to take another step. The sky continued to darken until it was almost the same color as the mountain.

The twins picked their way up the rocky slope, stepping carefully among uneven footholds and leaping across bottomless crevasses. They could feel unease in the air.

Not thirty minutes up the mountain, the wind picked up, bringing large snowflakes with it. The gray sky turned to black clouds, and the temperature plummeted.

"Hang on! We're in for a storm!" called Edgar, tightening his hood. Ellen did the same. Then the blizzard hit like a flock of attacking pigeons.

The wind was powerfully cold and so strong that the twins could lean into it without falling. Snow pelted them from all sides, stinging their eyes and exposed skin. This, plus the waist-high snowdrifts, made the going slow and difficult. But Pet had the worst of it. The snow was too deep, and the wind threatened to blow it away, so Ellen carried it, since Edgar's satchel was too packed with supplies for it to hitch a ride. Its eyelid kept freezing shut, and Ellen had to blow on it, using her warm breath to melt the persistent frost crystals.

Suddenly a particularly strong gale ripped Pet

from Ellen's arms, flinging it into the sky like a hairy snowball.

"Edgar, wait! Pet!" Ellen screamed at Edgar, who was a few paces ahead, but her voice was carried off by the wind. She threw a chunk of snow at him, and Edgar whipped around.

"Now is really not the time for a snowball fight!" he yelled.

"It's Pet, you dunce! Come on!"

The twins bounded through the snow as best they

could, calling out "Pet! Pet!" though they knew the creature had no way to answer their cries.

"What do we do, Brother?" asked Ellen.

"You're the one who let go, butterfingers," said Edgar.

"You try holding on to icy hair in the middle of a blizzard!"

"Well, visibility's terrible now. We're never going to find Pet in this storm. We'll have to make camp. Help me pitch the tent." Edgar pulled a patchwork tarp from his satchel. It caught the wind and billowed like a parachute; in a moment, it had ripped out of Edgar's grip and fluttered into the storming sky like a runaway ghost.

"Butterfingers, eh?" said Ellen, shaking her head. She grabbed the pickax from Edgar's satchel and started hacking into the side of a snowbank.

"What are you doing?" asked Edgar.

"Didn't you learn anything from that *Professor Paul* show Pet watches?" Ellen retorted. "When he's chasing tundra beetles and snow ferrets in the Arctic, he digs himself a shelter in the snow. If that crackpot can survive in this weather, so can we. Give me a hand, will you?"

The two whacked at the snow, slowly carving out

a narrow hovel. The winds worsened by the minute, numbing their hands, noses, and cheeks.

"Just a little deeper . . ." Ellen stabbed at the ground with her ax, and at that moment, the twins heard a rumble all around them.

"What—what was that?" said Edgar. They listened, but heard nothing but the howl of the wind.

"Um, Arctic thunder?" said Ellen. But then the earth quaked, knocking the twins to the ground. Edgar pointed up the mountain.

"Um, is it my imagination or is the mountain shrinking?"

Sure enough, what little they could see of the slope appeared to be dissolving into a cloud that was rushing straight for them.

"What is that?" asked Ellen, squinting. "A storm?"

"No!" Edgar shouted. "Avalanche! Run! Run!"

"No running," said Ellen. "Into the shelter!"

The twins dove inside the burrow just in time. The avalanche hit their hovel like a monster truck rally roaring directly over their heads. Edgar and Ellen covered their ears as they watched a torrent of snow rush past the opening. Their world rumbled around them.

"S-see?" called Ellen. "W-working p-per-perf-perf—"

That's when the roof of their shelter cracked and collapsed, squishing them flat.

8. A New Friend

A pale, bony hand poked through the smooth surface of the snow. To any tundra moles or snow ferrets watching, it might have looked like a buried corpse returning from the dead.

But it was no zombie invasion. It was Edgar.

"*Now* are we dead?" he called as he stuck his head out from the snow.

"I think death would be warmer," Ellen groaned. "But I can feel snow crammed down the back of my pajamas—I'd say we survived unscathed."

"Speak for yourself," said Edgar. He rubbed his face where the tumbling satchel had given him a black eye.

The twins looked around. The storm had abated, and the landscape had been wiped clean by the avalanche, giving the Glöggenheim a peaceful blanket of snow that belied the violence that had just occurred.

"Cripes, I hope Pet is okay," said Ellen.

Edgar scanned the mountain, then pointed down the slope. "Look!"

Pet was bounding across the snowdrifts toward them. It had a frantic look in its eye. In fact, it seemed to be waving a tendril in warning. And then—

Fwoop.

To Edgar and Ellen it looked as if the snow had reached up and dragged Pet under. The little creature had simply disappeared in a puff of powder.

"What in the name of Nod . . . ?" said Edgar.

Then a pillar of white rose from the spot where Pet had disappeared. It billowed up like a ghostly tower, rising seven feet above the ground, then began to drift over the snow toward them. From deep within came a doleful groan:

"Wwwaroooroooroo . . ."

"Sister? What is that?" Edgar backed away slowly.

"Whatever it is, Brother, I believe I'm going to run from it."

Ellen sped up the mountain face as fast as she could, Edgar just behind her. He glanced over his shoulder and saw the tower surge up after them.

"Wwwaroooorooroo . . ."

Ellen tripped over her own footies and splatted face-first into the snow.

Edgar tried to help her up, but then the shadow of the tower fell upon him. Up close, they saw it was more than just a spectral mound of snow: It was ice-matted fur, as if a polar bear were standing on its hind legs. But this was no mere polar bear.

"Brother?" Ellen felt herself lifted up off the ground by her footie and dangled in midair.

"Ellen! Don't. Move," hissed Edgar, who seemed very far below her.

"Don't move? Don't move?" Ellen called back, struggling wildly in the air. She flipped backward and forward, trying to see what had hold of her.

Edgar could see plainly what held his sister: a thick tendril of hair. But that was not the most remarkable thing. For Edgar now noticed that atop the mound of white hair was a great glassy orb. An eye. A single, blue eye.

"P-Pet?" he whispered.

At the sound of its name, Pet poked its eyeball

and a few strands of its black hair out of the middle of the pile of white fur. It reached desperately for help, but as suddenly as it appeared, it vanished, as if pulled underwater by a shark.

"Giant . . . evil . . . Pet?" said Edgar faintly.

"Get me down, Edgar!" yelled Ellen.

But in a moment, Edgar was hoisted just as high, wrapped in white hair, hanging upside down and helpless.

Edgar gulped. "Ellen, I believe we have found the Glögg."

9. Who Goes There?

"Hey! Put us down! What are you doing?" the twins cried, but the creature paid them no heed. It swished back up the snowy slope as easily as a toboggan. Now and again it would emit a low growl, certainly not a sound the twins had ever heard Pet make.

Though there was no path the twins could see, the creature sped across the ground with singular purpose. Soon the twins could make out a change in the surroundings. The featureless snow gave way

to jutting walls of rock. If possible, the landscape seemed even unfriendlier than before. The creature was taking them into the heart of the Glöggenheim.

It stopped in front of a large cavern rimmed with razor-sharp icicles, and dropped the twins unceremoniously on the ground. They attempted to get up, but the monster pushed them back down. From the cave, they heard a low cackle and a raspy voice, singing.

> *Peel their skins off, fry it twice,*
> *Pack the bones in snow and ice,*
> *Pudding says it's time to eat,*
> *How I love the stench of meat!*

The twins exchanged horrified looks. They could see a figure coming toward them from deep inside the cave.

"What have you brought me, Yehti, my lovely?" the raspy voice asked. It was a woman, only the oldest, ugliest, most decrepit woman the twins had ever seen. Her hair, or what was left of it, fell in straggly gray lumps to her shoulders, but her scalp was covered in bald patches, as if the hair had been yanked out. Her eye sockets sank so deeply into her skull, it was difficult to see the whites of her eyes, and her skin was paler than the twins'. She was so wrinkled that, Edgar thought, if there were such a thing as a white prune, this is what it would look like.

Her back hunched, and she wore a ratty fur coat and stockings, which didn't seem like enough protection from the negative temperatures. But if she was cold, she did not show it. She approached the twins curiously, as though she had never seen children before.

"What are these cubs, I wonder?" she muttered, circling like a hyena.

"We're snow inspectors," said Ellen. "Good news! Looks like your snow passed the test. So, I suppose we should be getting back—"

"They talk, they squawk, they belly-gawk," the woman said.

"What's a belly-gawk?" Edgar whispered.

"Who knows?" Ellen mumbled back. "Cripes, I thought we had to be worried about the Glögg. . . ."

At the sound of the name, the woman whipped a sharpened icicle from her fur and held it to Ellen's neck. She moved faster than either twin thought possible.

"What do you know of Glögg?" she demanded, staring straight at Ellen. For the first time, Ellen noticed that her eyes went in different directions.

"N-Not much," Ellen stammered. "Just that's it's very nice. And, um, that it doesn't like to eat helpless children."

"Spies! Spies!" The old woman's eyes bulged. "Spies come to steal the pudding!" At this the monster behind them grabbed the twins and hoisted them back into the air, growling ferociously.

"We don't want any pudding!" Edgar shouted. "I swear, no pudding!"

"Lady, I'm telling you, we are not the enemy," Ellen called out. "We're not going to steal any, er, pudding from you. We're on a mission to save the world!"

"And you tell me I exaggerate," Edgar muttered.

"No, no, pudding says no," said the woman. And then she cracked each of them on the head with the icicle, and all went black.

10. The Glögg

Ellen woke first. She was hanging upside down, her feet encased in the cavern's icy roof. Not far off, Edgar hung in the same manner. Ellen's head swam: She wasn't sure whether it was from being upside down or from being whacked with an icicle. Probably both. The old woman knelt off to the side, making a fire.

"Lady, please listen to me," Ellen said. "We don't want anything from you."

"The spies, the spies, they cries, they cries, then they dies, they dies," the woman sang.

"Is that the Glögg outside? That big monster thing?" Ellen continued, trying not to think about that last bit of the hag's song.

"Ha! That is Yehti. You seek Glögg? You have found her. Uta Glögg. That is I."

"You're—Glögg is a human?" Ellen said. *"Not* the monster . . ."

"Yehti brings me pretty presents," said Uta Glögg. Then she peered into Ellen's face. "Some not so pretty—but still, a present nonetheless."

Uta Glögg stoked the fire. "Yehti is happy now it can stalk new prey," Uta Glögg continued. "Its own kin makes suitable quarry, I think."

"Its kin. You mean Pet?" Ellen demanded. "The little hairball?"

"Surprising to find that Yehti has family, but that is the pudding for you. Full of surprises," said Uta Glögg. "Full of secrets. And those secrets will all be mine, yes, they will."

She picked up a cup of something that looked remarkably like the balm Ellen had known in Nod's Limbs, though this goop was light blue like a robin's egg, not white. She swirled the goop and took a swig.

"Not too much, not too little," Uta Glögg said

absently. "Good at jacks, bad at skittles . . ."

Then she noticed Ellen watching her intently.

"Recognize this, do you?" said the old woman as she held the cup to Ellen's face. "Yes, I thought so, I thought so. Uta knows there's more pudding out there. And she will find it. Now tell me: Where are you from? Where can I find more pudding?"

"Look, lady, we know a thing or two about this pudding of yours. Once people discover this stuff lets them live forever, it makes them a little obsessed. Power hungry. Mad."

"I'm not mad!" Uta Glögg snapped. "There's no one mad here!" She came eyeball to eyeball with Ellen. "If I don't make the pudding mine, whelps like you will get it first. I won't let you, I won't!"

With that she stormed deeper into the cave, beyond the torchlight.

"Edgar, Edgar, wake up!" Ellen hissed at her brother. He was starting to come to.

"Oh, walnuts," he moaned, clutching his head.

"Edgar, that crazy lady is hoarding balm!"

"Why," asked Edgar in a pained voice, "are we spending so much time unconscious?"

"Pull it together, Brother! Uta said that other Pet is out there hunting its 'kin.' I think that means it's trying to make a meal of *our* Pet."

"So it is a Pet—or a Pilosoculus, or *ithune*, or whatever you call them. Maybe every balm spring comes equipped with its very own Pet!"

"Well, this one's not so mild-mannered as ours. And that crone is loopier than Miles Knightleigh on a sugar high, and I don't want to know what she plans to do with us."

"If I could just reach my satchel . . ." Edgar stretched his hand toward the bag, lying on the cavern floor, but it was just out of reach.

"Pudding says to play with fire," said Uta Glögg, appearing in front of Ellen. She held out a torch to Ellen's face. "They're waking and scheming, quaking and screaming. . . ."

"Hey, get that away from me!" shrieked Ellen, but Uta Glögg grabbed one of her pigtails and brought the torch so close to her, it singed Ellen's eyelashes. "Edgar, help!"

Edgar struggled as wildly as Ellen but could not break free. Suddenly, a small, hairy ball scrambled into the cave, Yehti chasing right behind it.

"Pet!" cried Edgar. "Quick, my satchel!"

Pet dove for Edgar's satchel and somersaulted across the top. As it skimmed the surface it plucked a ratchet wrench from the junk and flicked it to Edgar. Yehti pounced, but tripped over the satchel as Pet skittered off. Edgar whacked at the ice with the steel tool while Pet raced back across the cavern and through Uta Glögg's legs. Yehti plunged after, knocking into Uta, who went sprawling. As Uta fell, Ellen seized the torch from her hand and thrust it at the ice encasing her feet. In a moment, she tumbled to the floor. Seconds later Edgar chiseled himself free as well, grabbed his satchel, and the two of them stumbled to the cavern entrance where Pet waited.

As Uta Glögg howled and Yehti roared, Edgar, Ellen, and Pet escaped down the hill as fast as Arctic hares, singing as they ran:

> Hurry, flurry, don't look back!
> Flee from Yehti's swift attack,
> Or face that raving maniac
> And in her clutches caught!
> Faster, faster down, but oh!
> Our footies slowed by deep'ning snow!
> The safety of the woods below
> May be our only shot!

11. The Best Laid Traps

They half ran, half tumbled down the slope of the Glöggenheim until they reached the pine grove at the edge of Mudjut Meadow. They looked back, but neither Uta Glögg nor Yehti was following them. That still did not stop Pet from cowering behind Ellen for extra safety.

"She . . . she was going to burn me alive!" Ellen panted.

"What do we do now?" asked Edgar, after he'd caught his breath.

"We're definitely in the right spot," said Ellen. "The balm spring must be deeper in that cave of hers."

"So if Stephanie left Frøsthaven to find this place, why hasn't she had the privilege of meeting our two new friends?" asked Edgar.

"Who says she hasn't? Maybe she's Yehti food by now," mused Ellen. "Though I didn't see her head mounted on the wall back there. Pity."

Edgar picked up the shivering Pet. "This is all so weird. Did you know you had a giant snow beast for a cousin, Pet?" The little creature shook its eyeball.

"If that Uta Glögg has been eating balm, who

knows how long it's kept her alive?" said Ellen.

"Sister, hasn't the novelty of stuff like this worn off since the first time we found a two-hundred-year-old person kicking around?" asked Edgar.

"You'd think so, wouldn't you?" Ellen shook her head. "But we should find out for sure what happened to Stephanie. Which means, yeesh, we'll have to go back in there to gather clues."

"Have *you* gone mental?" asked Edgar. "We were almost charcoal back there."

"Which is why we have to trap Yehti first. We can handle Uta if her muscle is out of the way."

Edgar looked doubtfully at his satchel. "I'm pretty sure I don't have anything big enough in here."

The twins looked across the meadow, where they saw the sparkling spires of Frøsthaven swirling into the air like glass pussy willows.

"Back to Frosting-haven?" said Edgar.

"Yes. Unless I get a whiff of *derflootle* first," said Ellen. She cradled her aching stomach.

12. Long Distance

"I hope Nod and Dahlia are okay," said Ellen as they walked toward town. The last twenty-four hours had been so eventful, it seemed like ages since she'd even thought of them. "Maybe we should try to contact Miles and see if Nod's reported in."

"Not a bad idea," said Edgar.

They agreed to split up. Edgar would contact home since he was adept at hacking into electronic systems like phone cables. Ellen and Pet, meanwhile, would scour the town junkyard, a clean and orderly refuse dump on the outskirts of Frøsthaven. Most people tend to avoid places as distasteful as junkyards, but to Edgar and Ellen, they had always been supermarkets of surprising supplies. Most of their best pranks had been hatched among junk, and perhaps today would be no different.

Edgar hummed to himself as he went about his assignment. Wielding a pocket knife, an oscilloscope, a beat-up walkie-talkie, three brass cufflinks, and a toothpick (all of which he had produced from his overstuffed satchel), he shinnied up the biggest telephone pole he could find and went to work.

To an accomplished schemer like Edgar, it was

really just a matter of bifurcating the alternating gyratic capacitor signal and diverting the current into his walkie handset. Just like that, he was able to get an open line and replicate a dialed phone number using the sublimated frequencies of bioelectrical feedback.

"Piece of cake," said Edgar as he heard a ring on the line.

"Dartjool monka hi?" said a voice on the other end.

"Uh, sorry, wrong number," said Edgar, and he hung up. He recalibrated his dial-tone controls by smacking them thrice with a wrench. As it turned out, tapping into a phone line was far trickier than he had thought, especially given that he had never quite finished the phone company pamphlet from which he had gleaned his knowledge of the trade. In all, he felt lucky that within the hour, he had managed to contact the front desk of a pool hall in Smelterburg that could transfer him to a Nod's Limbs operator who could patch him in to his old house.

The phone rang: once, twice, three times.

"Come on," said Edgar.

Finally, on the fifth ring, a breathless voice answered.

"Hello, Nod residence. Who may I ask is calling?" Miles Knightleigh's voice crackled over the receiver. Edgar heard a commotion in the background. Miles yelled, "Hey, fingers are not for biting!"

"It's Edgar, Miles. What's going on?"

"Edgar! Omigosh am I glad to hear from you!" bubbled Miles. "I've been super worried about—no! No! That's no way for a potted plant to behave!"

Wham, wham, wham!

"Miles, is everything okay?"

"Okeydokey, fearless leader!" Miles chirped. "Just feeding Ellen's plants."

"That doesn't sound like feeding. It sounds like beating."

"I'm giving Gustav his afternoon croaking beetle. Yow! Gustav! What did we say about eating my foot? Ow, ow—ha ha ha—that tickles!"

"Miles, has Nod returned yet?"

"No, which is too bad. I could sure use his help getting my hat back from Morella. I didn't know pitcher plants snacked on clothing. Do you think she has a grudge against cotton plants?"

"Focus, Miles! Have you heard from Nod at all?"

"Oh! Nod's homing raven Grip just arrived today. Let me get the note." More *whacks* and *bams* came from the other end, then Miles got back on the line. "It says, 'Taking longer than planned. Caught sniff of Heimertz Circus. Stephanie not working alone, but can't tell who's working with her. Don't let her get her hands on any more balm. Research suggests mixing balm from different springs could have disastrous results. Out.' Does any of that make sense to you, Edgar?"

"Maybe," said Edgar. His brow furrowed. "If you get a chance to send word to Nod, tell him we're on Stephanie's trail, but we haven't found her yet. Miles, I just want to warn you—there's a chance she's already dead."

There was silence on the other end for a minute, then Miles said only, "Stephie knows how to take care of Stephie."

"Yes, she does," said Edgar. "And there's more. We found a balm spring up here. It's guarded by a crazy old coot and a seven-foot snow beast that seems to be a relative of Pet's."

"Wow, another Pet?" Miles exclaimed. "Pet must be so excited! Family!"

"Family with homicidal tendencies. You could relate, Miles," Edgar added, realizing the parallels between Yehti and the rest of the Knightleigh clan.

"You said it—Gustav, put me down!"

"Are you sure you have this under control?" said Edgar.

"Are you kidding? I'm Miles Knightleigh!" said Miles. "Let me know when you save the world! Whoa! Bad man-eating plant! Bad man-eating pla—"

The line went dead. Edgar unhooked his home-made phone and wriggled down the telephone pole.

13. Ring-a-Ding-Ding

Edgar caught up to his sister and Pet in front of the town's bell tower.

"I've got bad news," he told them. "I think I know what Stephanie's up to. Or, at least, partly. Nod left word that *combining* balms could prove to be disastrous—maybe that's why she's after multiple balms. To combine them into some sort of super-weapon."

Ellen's jaw dropped. "The letters Steph wrote on the wall. NL plus BD. Nod's Limbs plus Black Diamond. She's referring to the balms found in each place."

"There were other letters after those."

"They must stand for the next places she intends to go."

"So there are at least four springs, and she seems to know where they are, since she has codes for them. Great. I really hope Yehti got her. How'd you two do?"

It seemed Ellen and Pet had little to show for their effort. Pet had scrounged up an ancient hoop skirt, and Ellen a busted birdcage, but neither seemed likely to contain Yehti, let alone an enraged Stephanie.

Ellen had recalled once capturing Heimertz by using the metal rings of a barrel, but after Pet did some speedy reconnaissance around town, they learned that all the barrels of Frøsthaven were carved of ice and shaped like flowerpots—not sturdy enough to capture a snow monster, abominable or otherwise.

"The Arctic has the *worst* trash," Ellen lamented, plopping onto the ground in front of the tower.

"We could dig a pit trap," suggested Edgar.

"We'd need dynamite to get through all that rock," said Ellen. "Too loud."

"Well, we could eject Yehti off the mountain with a concealed catapult."

"Too complicated."

"Well then, let's just drop an anvil on its noggin."

"Drop an anvil? I don't know, we'd have to be really precise. . . ." Ellen leaned back against the bell tower in deep thought. As she did so, she looked up at the sky. Then she gasped and pointed straight up. "Not just *on* its noggin—*over* it!"

Edgar followed her pointing finger. "What, a cloud? You can't drop a cloud on someone and expect to—"

"I'm not pointing at the sky," said Ellen. "I'm

pointing at the top of the bell tower!"

"What, are you a tourist now?" said Edgar. "Maybe we should get a postcard."

"No, genius, *the bell*. The perfect cage!" Ellen turned her brother's head to a sign hanging at the entrance to the tower.

THE BLACK DIAMOND BELL TOWER MUSEUM
COME SEE THE LEGEND ITSELF!

"Really?" asked Edgar.

"Any bell fit for this tower is going to be big enough to swallow that monster like a marshmallow."

"It could be," Edgar replied, cracking his knuckles. "Let's take a look—maybe case the place first."

But when he pushed open the entrance doors of the museum, a cascade of tinkling chimes and jangling bells greeted their arrival.

"So much for stealth," muttered Ellen.

"*Guud kloost!* Welcome to the museum!" piped a young woman. She stood behind a counter stacked with miniature bell towers and books with titles such as *The Chime of Our Lives* and *To Bell and Back*.

"My name is Lilja, and I'll be your museum guide today."

Before Edgar and Ellen could sneak out the door and try a less conspicuous entrance, Lilja had bounded up to them and seized their hands in a hearty shake.

"Er, thanks, Lil, but we don't need a guide," said Ellen. "We just wanted to see this bell of yours."

"Of course you do!" Lilja exclaimed. "It's the charmingest bell in the Arctic Circle! I'm sorry to tell you, though"—here she pointed at something just behind them on the floor—"we don't allow dogs inside."

"Dogs?" said Ellen. "Oh, Pet! Okay, Pet, you heard her, you stay outside and sniff a fire hydrant or something. There's a good doggy. And, uh," she added in a whisper, "try to get your hair on a sled. And maybe a big blanket. We're going to need a way to sneak this thing out of town."

Pet shot her an angry look as it shuffled outside. It slammed the door shut with its tendrils.

Lilja the tour guide led Edgar and Ellen into the next room. It appeared to be empty, but when she hit a switch, a thousand watts of blinding light hit a bell hanging from a sturdy beam. But instead of illuminating a mass of bronze, the light hit the surface of the crystalline bell, refracting into countless little rainbows.

"It's made of ice!" moaned Ellen. "Of all the rotten luck—"

"The best kind of ice." Lilja winked at Ellen. "Diamond! This bell was hand-crafted from the famous Black Diamond from which the glacier takes its name, the biggest diamond in the world, found right here in Snorgpeke Mountain!"

Edgar stroked his chin. "And as everyone knows," he said, "diamonds are the *hardest substance on Earth.*"

"That's right!" said Lilja. "Nearly unbreakable! It took a hundred jewelers and two thousand *snargs* of dynamite to finally carve this most perfect of bells!"

"And how convenient you keep it on the ground floor," said Edgar. "Easier for us to, uh, *admire* it."

"Actually it came out of the tower the day it was installed, the day of the Breaking," said Lilja. "But you probably already know that. It's the most famous story for five thousand *crickles*!"

"Pretend we live five thousand and one *crickles* away," said Ellen. "Did the bell break?"

"Not the bell—the mountain!" said Lilja. Her

voice softened but lost none of its dramatic style, as if she were telling a ghost story. "It was almost two hundred years ago. Five years after Kommodore Frøstblatt discovered the Black Diamond and founded Frøsthaven. The town celebrated its anniversary with a grand festival, at which the crowning moment was to be the inaugural ringing of the new diamond bell. After the children danced their traditional *skipderloo* and everyone had their fill of *derflootle*, the kommodore himself walked to the top of the bell tower, and to a hail of applause and cheers, he gave the bell pull a mighty heave, and . . ."

"And . . . ?" asked Ellen.

"And the bell rang, of course," said Lilja.

Edgar looked at Ellen and rolled his eyes. "Well, that's a heck of a story, Lil, but if you don't mind, we're going to—"

"*Diiiiiiiiiing!*" said Lilja loudly. "*Diiiiiiiiiing!* It was the purest tone anyone had ever heard, a resonance of raw, primal sound, as powerful and complex as the diamond itself."

"Really, that'll do—" began Ellen.

"*BOOOOOOM!*" Lilja thundered. She gestured so wildly, Edgar was forced to duck. "The sound of the diamond bell traveled like an explosion, rebounding upon itself, growing louder and louder. It reverberated off the buildings, off the trees, and off Snorgpeke itself! The vibrations of this beautiful bell were exactly—*exactly!*—attuned to the very heart of the mountain. And as soon as the last undulations died away, the mountain rumbled and quivered and at last gave way—*cracka-cracka-BOOM-ba!*—sending a monstrous avalanche of snow and rock upon the town."

"Whoa," said the twins.

"The town was buried, the five-year-old buildings all destroyed, the spark of Frøsthaven almost utterly wiped off the face of the Earth." Lilja's voice was a whisper, and she hung her head low against her chest.

"This story got pretty good," said Ellen.

"Oh, we're all better now," said Lilja cheerily. "They took the clapper out of the bell right away, of course, and it's never been rung since. And that's the story of the Breaking."

14. Borrowed Jewels

Edgar and Ellen praised Lilja for her storytelling and assured her the tale was the most moving they'd ever heard. Ellen expressed her amazement that Lilja wasn't exhausted from all that effort, and Lilja agreed she could do with a glass of orange juice and a little nap. The twins promised her they would watch the museum for a while if she wanted to go home and get some rest. After a few moments of protest, she agreed.

"I thought she'd never leave," said Edgar, waving after her.

"Let's move," said Ellen. She tugged a pigtail as she regarded the bell. Though the ceiling was not terribly high, the bell was affixed firmly to the steel beam. "How do we get it down?"

"Well, this is a museum isn't it?" said Edgar. "This place is probably full of bell-related gear they used to haul this thing around."

Edgar was right: Several glass cases contained useful tools with labels such as ORIGINAL HOISTING CHAIN and FRØSTBLATT'S HAND-WHITTLED WINCH. Though quite old, these items looked ideally suited for moving the bell (as well as securing it in their trap), and Edgar emptied the cases. They were unlocked, as one might expect in a trusting town like Frøsthaven, and they included seemingly useful items such as iron spikes, box-ended spanners, and an exquisite silver hammer. Edgar could never resist antique hand tools.

Using the winch, the hoisting chain, and an improvised pulley made from Edgar's favorite iron shackles, the twins unhooked the enormous bell from its perch and lowered it to the floor. Even with the tools, the bell was incredibly heavy and unwieldy; it swung violently several times, knocking over Edgar twice and nearly chipping Ellen's tooth. At last they settled the great beast onto its side—careful to avoid hitting it and making it ring—and rolled it toward the doors.

"How are we going to get this out of town without being noticed?" asked Ellen.

"You're the smooth talker," said Edgar. "If someone stops us, charm them."

"Oh, that plan sounds foolproof. Let's see if Pet found anything useful." She and Edgar poked their heads out the door and called for their friend.

Pet rounded a corner and waved a tendril, beckoning them to follow.

The twins tiptoed around the corner of the bell tower. Pet eagerly hopped up and down, pointing at a tall red sleigh. Two people, a man and a woman, were harnessing a team of walruses to it and preparing to ride. They were impeccably dressed. In fact, they could be considered fashion daredevils in a town like Frøsthaven. The woman wore an ocher-and-vermillion bodysuit with more buckles than a shipload of buccaneers, while the man's otherwise sensible parka was festooned with furry poms; his calf-high boots were made of polar bear fur, giving his legs the shaggy appearance of a Clydesdale draft horse.

"Good job, Pet," whispered Ellen. "These two look even flakier than the usual snowflakes in this town. Getting rid of them should be easy."

But Pet continued to wave its hairs, and it dipped one tendril in the snow and wrote:

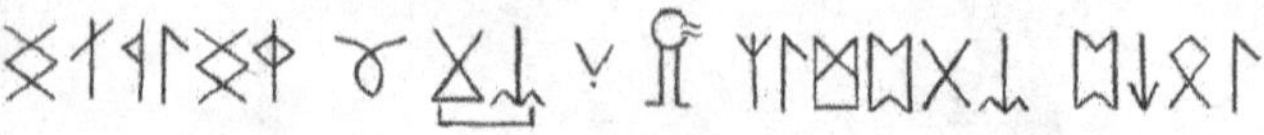 [8]

"Listen?" read Ellen. "Listen to what?"

Then the woman spoke. "This place is positively horrid, Nils! It's like a giant curio cabinet full of tacky glass figurines!"

Edgar frowned. "I've heard that voice before."

The man answered her: "You can see why my parents left, Nora dear. These people have created an artificial environment to resurrect a past that never existed! Now, if they had only seen the upside-down opera house you and I designed in Belmopan . . ."

"Nils? Nora? Oh, cripes," said Ellen. "It's those two uppity architects, Edgar—the ones who came to Nod's Limbs with Knightleigh's big tourist program. . . ."

"Wait, really?" Edgar brightened. "That Nils was screaming like a howler monkey by the end of our tour!"

"Suddenly the problem of getting rid of them isn't so problematic," said Ellen with a smile. She pulled a slightly greasy cheesecloth from Edgar's satchel. "I have a wonderful, ridiculous idea."

"This town needs to modernize, that's what it needs," continued Nora deGroot as she buckled a harness. "Everything is *charmingest* this and *quaintest* that. These provincial attitudes are holding back progress!"

"Quite agreed," said Nils deGroot, fumbling with a walrus of his own. "If we could encourage them to begin a massive public works campaign, we could— Oh, hello, what's that sound?"

A ghostly moan floated down from seemingly nowhere.

"Oooh. Oooooh!"

"Nils, is that some sort of walrus call? Or is it— *Oh my heavens!*"

Nora deGroot fell back. What looked like a puff of gray smoke was wafting toward them. It might have been a localized patch of fog, except for how it moved: bubbling, roiling, swaying. The peculiar cloud moved with purpose toward the deGroots. More unnerving still, it *talked.*

"Oooh! Nils deGroot! You have been bad. Very bad!" came a voice from the quivering cloud.

Nils deGroot paled. "What—what— How do you know my name? What are you?"

"I am Borsk—Borsk the noble polar bear of the southern slopes. I was killed—murdered!—to make those boots you wear."

Nils and Nora deGroot clutched each other. Nils stammered, "I—I thought they were synthetic fur!"

"Synthetic? Bah!" The cloud shook violently. *"It is my flesh you wear, Nils. My flesh! And I have come to get it back!"*

"We have angered an animal totem, Nils! Our karma is tainted!"

"Run, Nora, run!" screamed Nils de Groot, kicking off his boots as he stumbled away. "We'll cleanse our karma in an ice bath!"

The two architects raced off, leaving behind a perfectly good walrus-drawn sleigh.

Ellen pulled off the cheesecloth sheet from her and her brother's heads. "That was *too* easy."

"Yes, they could have given us a small challenge at least," said Edgar.

They grabbed the reins and led the waddling walruses to the front door of the museum. They had the world's biggest diamond to steal, and the world's most expensive trap to set.

15. To Catch the Abominable

Using the deGroots' sleigh, the twins transported the enormous diamond bell and the rest of their loot across Mudjut Meadow. Pet returned from a quick reconnaissance trip up the Glöggenheim and reported that there were no fresh footprints (or hair tracks) outside the cave.

"Either that's a good sign because they're inside napping . . . ," said Ellen.

". . . or a bad sign because they've been out hunting for us and are due to come back soon," said Edgar.

"Well, what's life without a few risks?" sighed Ellen.

The walruses labored as best they could up the slope. As they neared the cave entrance, the steep terrain tilted the sleigh too far, and the bell rolled out onto a bed of snow, nearly tumbling into a deep ravine. The twins knew they'd have to do the rest themselves.

They freed the walruses, who slid on their bellies down the slope.

"This winch can haul the bell the rest of the way up," said Edgar,

So he and his sister carried the winch up past the mouth of the cave while Pet dragged Edgar's satchel. The cave itself was tucked under an outcropping of rock, so that a ledge jutted overhead. This gave the cave protection from avalanches, but more impor-tant, it also gave the twins the perfect platform from which to dangle the bell.

When they finally reached this outcropping, they

looked downhill and could clearly see the bell—
as well as their footprints in the snow, leaving an
unmistakable trail to their hiding spot.

"There's no way this is going to work," Ellen
muttered.

"Have a little faith," said Edgar. "If not in me, at
least in *physics*."

A winch is a handy tool, and the two-hundred-
year-old model they had carried with them was an
exceptionally powerful one. The post was about half
a Heimertz wide, and the handles were as thick as
basbøl bats. Hauling the bell up the hill would be
as easy as winding a thread on a spool—perhaps a
very, very heavy thread—but first the winch needed
to be secured to the rock. Pet fished a mallet from
the satchel, as well as the recently borrowed iron
spikes. As Edgar raised the mallet to drive the first
spike, he froze.

"The sound of all this hammering will resonate
in the cave," he said. "Do I risk it?"

"We've come all this way!" Ellen said. "Don't let
the fear of impending doom stop you *now*."

Still, Edgar hesitated. At last he raised the mallet for a mighty blow, and as he did so, he heard a
growl.

Edgar froze yet again. The growl came from the mouth of the cave beneath them. A moment later they saw Yehti shuffle out into the open, snuffling as if it had caught the scent of something in the wind. Had the bell been in position, it would have been the perfect moment to trigger the trap.

But Yehti's snuffling got louder and louder. Was it about to discover the twins hiding just a few feet overhead?

Edgar whispered to his sister, "Who's faster? Me or you?"

Ellen smirked. "Neither," she whispered back. "Pet."

She picked up Pet by the scruff, and looked it in the eyeball. "Run," she whispered, and with that she tossed the creature off the ledge. It landed right in front of Yehti.

"ROWWWR!" roared the snow monster as it lunged for Pet. Pet darted aside, then dashed off. Yehti pursued. Pet led the creature back and forth in front of the cave, and the great hairy pursuer howled in fury.

Each time Yehti roared, however, Edgar brought down the mallet. The sounds of his work were completely concealed by the ruckus below them.

Edgar was done in just a minute. In that time,

Pet had chased Yehti in such a zigzagged path that the twins' footprints up the slope were completely obscured. Only a bloodhound could have found where the small footie-pajama prints diverged from the confusion of swishes and sweeps.

Pet seemed to be tiring, and every lunge Yehti made came closer to connecting with Pet's trailing tendrils. After one swipe knocked Pet end over end into a sharp rock, it had had enough. It leaped to the top of the rock and turned to face its pursuer. It raised two tendrils like little fists and made a "come and get it" gesture—and the snow monster seemed ready to oblige.

The twins didn't know what to do.

"Yehti!" bellowed Uta Glögg from the cave. "Yehti, where are you?"

The big white beast stopped in its tracks and turned toward the woman's voice. Pet skittered into a crevice.

"Get in here, you great lump!" called Uta Glögg. "Our visitors need tending to."

Yehti howled a plaintive protest, like a child called to supper in the middle of his favorite game. When it looked back and saw Pet had escaped, it stomped a tuft of hair and growled.

"Chasing Arctic hares again?" barked the old woman. "You'll get back to your hobbies later. We have work to do. *Now!*"

Yehti let out a low, gurgling growl and followed Uta Glögg back inside the cave.

"Phew," breathed Edgar. "That was close."

"Visitors?" said Ellen.

Within minutes they had the chain attached to the bell and were hauling it up the mountainside with the help of the winch. With every heave on the handles, the bell inched up the slope. When they had at last hoisted the bell above the cave, all that remained was to attach it to a hair-trigger trip wire that would engage when the monster walked out from the cave entrance. Fortunately, hair-trigger trip wires were standard fare for accomplished pranksters like Edgar and Ellen.

"Is it a Double Moriarty slipknot?" asked Ellen, making the final connection with the trip wire. "Or the Three-Fingered Violinist?"

"The Inverted Krakow," said Edgar. "You should know that."

"Oh, yeah," said Ellen, hastily tying off the wire. "That should do it. Now, are we going in there or what?"

16. Into the Belly

Edgar wanted to wait and watch the trap, but Ellen was too eager to see if Stephanie had stumbled into Uta Glögg's clutches.

"The only reason I'm agreeing to this," said Edgar after much begging and pleading, "is it might actually save us time if Yehti sees us—then we could lead it back to the trap. Just leap over the trip wire when you run out of the cave."

"Leap over the wire, right, right," said Ellen. "Now, can we go?"

Edgar looked at Pet, who shook its eyeball in an emphatic no.

"Fine, Pet, you stand watch," said Edgar. "Guard my satchel like it's the most precious thing on Earth—even more so than your television."

Pet gave a little salute, then hopped in the satchel. It shaded its eyelid with a tendril and did its best imitation of a lookout in the crow's nest of a whaling ship.

"Quit clowning, Pet! This is my *satchel* we're talking about!"

Pet shrugged and hunkered down farther amid the knickknacks in the satchel.

"Let's just get this over with," Edgar huffed.

As Edgar and Ellen crept deeper into the darkness of the cave, they could see a flicker of illumination far in the distance, which helped them navigate the maze of tunnels that branched off all around them.

"This is the room where Uta had us strung up like sausages," whispered Edgar. "Wouldn't she do the same to Stephanie if she'd captured her?"

"Uta was going to 'tend to her visitors,'" said Ellen quietly. "Maybe 'tend to' is an Arctic way of saying 'eat.'"

"*Visitors*. That plural is troublesome. Who could be with Stephanie?" mused Edgar. "By the time she left Nod's Limbs she didn't have any friends left. I don't know, this whole thing stinks."

Soon they got a whiff of a familiar, distinctive odor that did indeed stink: the balm. The tunnel banked steeply forward, and they had to take care not to slip on the icy floor. With every step down the sheer trail, the scent grew stronger.

As they descended into the bowels of the mountain, the twins could hear voices.

"Heave, then!" cried one. "Got lots of this stuff to move!"

"Give a hand, will you?" said another. "My bucket's full!"

"That doesn't sound like Uta or Stephanie," Edgar whispered to Ellen. "Is someone else on to the balm—oof!"

Edgar stepped too quickly on a slick patch of ice and his feet flew out from underneath him. He grabbed onto Ellen to stop his fall but only pulled her down with him, and together they slid down the icy path straight into a large cavern.

The place reeked of balm, and the twins could see the spring glooping and gurgling on the other side of the hollow.

Their cover blown, the twins wobbled to their feet to face down these new foes holding bright lanterns and buckets filled with the bluish balm. But when the twins saw the faces of their enemies, they could not speak. It was too impossible.

17. Reunion

Five sets of eyes blinked back at the twins. They were all there: Imogen, ringmaster-in-training and leader of the crew; Gonzalo, the cowboy clown, as quick with a joke as he was with his lasso; Mab and Merrick, sibling tightrope walkers and the youngest members of the world-renowned Hei-Flyers trapeze act; and little Phoebe, the insect tamer. Together, they were the Midway Irregulars, the young band of circus mischief-makers that the twins had once called friends.

But it had ended badly, all that time ago. Edgar and Ellen had been framed, and the Heimertz clan tricked into thinking the twins had betrayed the circus.

Had all been forgiven?

"Edgar!" Phoebe shouted, and she ran up and threw her arms around him. "I missed you *so much*!"

"You—you did?" Edgar asked. "Listen, Phoebe, I'm really sorry I lost your flants. . . ."

"No worries," said Phoebe. "They deserve to be free, flying in the great wide open, meeting other flant colonies."

"That's very understanding of you," said Edgar.

"Howdy, ma'am," said Gonzalo, tipping his hat to Ellen. "I'm happier to see you than a turkey on a Sunday dinner table!"

"You are?" said Ellen. "That's good. I guess. So you're not still mad at us about the whole big top–collapsing thing?"

"Gosh, no!" said Mab.

"Wasn't your fault," said Merrick.

"We know it was that dirty mollusk Ormond who framed you," said Imogen. "When Benedict woke up, he told us the whole story."

"We're glad Benedict's okay," said Edgar quickly, remembering that the last time he and Ellen had seen the eccentric, elderly ringmaster, he had been

unconscious and close to death. "We know he and Nod have been pen pals."

"They sure are!" said Gonzalo. "Ol' Uncle B. told us how your house collapsed and how that old-timer Nod popped out of the ground like a dandelion in a patch of Texas clover. Boy howdy, is that a whopper of a tale!"

"But what are you doing *here*?" asked Ellen. "Have you seen Uta Glögg? And that giant white Pet—I mean, *ithune*?" she corrected herself, using the term the circus people gave the one-eyed creatures.

"Where are they, anyway?" asked Edgar. "We're pretty exposed down here, and I don't want another run-in with that Yehti thing."

"I wouldn't worry about ol' Uta," said Imogen. "She's occupied at the moment."

"But Stephanie!" said Ellen. "Stephanie Knightleigh is looking for this place. If Yehti doesn't have

her yet, she could be here any moment."

"Oh, we know all about Stephanie," said Imogen, "and her schemes."

"Excellent," said Edgar. "So what's the plan?"

"Simple," said Imogen, and, quick as a whip, Gonzalo had snared both twins with his lasso. "We have to kill you."

18. Cry Me a River

"Kill us?" cried Edgar. "But I thought you *forgave* us!"

"All is forgiven," said Merrick.

"But we have our orders," said Mab.

"Orders? Whose orders?" said Ellen.

"Boss lady's," said Gonzalo as he lashed each twin tight in a separate set of ropes. He took special care to tie their hands tight behind their backs so they couldn't reach the knots. "By golly, you sure were a humdinger of an escape artist, Edgar. The best, I'll reckon! Exceptin' for today. T'aint no one can wriggle out of these here escape-proof knots."

A worried look passed over Edgar's face as he

tested his bonds and found them to be quite secure.

As Gonzalo started dragging them up the path, Edgar and Ellen noticed that the rest of the Irregulars carried buckets full of balm.

"What is this?" said Ellen. "Are you harvesting balm now too? Your family is supposed to *protect* it!"

"All is done for a reason," said Imogen. "Hush, now."

"I will not hush!" cried Ellen. "I will not— *mmmph.*" Phoebe wrapped a gag over Ellen's mouth and tied it tightly. Then she patted Edgar on the head.

"Good Edgar, don't make a sound, or I'll have to do the same to you," she said sweetly.

Gonzalo led the twins to a chamber near the cave mouth and pushed them to the ground.

"So how do we kill 'em?" he asked Imogen.

"Let's ask the boss," she replied. "But not yet. She's telling her bedtime stories."

Sure enough, the twins heard murmuring in a corner of the chamber. Uta Glögg sat on the ground, reading from a large, ragged book. In front of her sat Yehti. The creature wore a strange sponge strapped under its eye and appeared to be listening raptly to her creaky voice.

". . . and then the kittens were forced to flee from their warm nest in the barn," Uta Glögg read. "'Skitter! Skatter!' screeched Crag the Owl. 'Ye shan't outrun the likes of me, Binky, Plinky, and Mot!'"

The twins glanced at each other.

"This is weird," said Edgar. Ellen nodded emphatically.

"Binky, Plinky, and Mot ran and ran and ran, as fast as their wee kitten legs could carry them," Uta continued. "They came to a stream that had no boat nor bridge. 'How shall we cross?' cried Binky. 'We will have to swim!' wailed Plinky. 'But the water is ever so cold!' moaned Mot. But evil Crag the Owl was swooping in, and there was naught to do but plunge into the rushing current, so that's what the little kittens did. They waded in up to their little necks, paddled with their little paws, and hoped for the best. Splash, splash, splash, across the river, swam Binky, Plinky, and Mot. But when they were almost to the other side, they saw a terrible sight! Three huge rabid dogs prowled the opposite bank. No escape! No escape for our kittens three! And they drowned!"

"Cripes," Edgar whispered. "Who wrote that? Mother Gruesome?" Ellen shrugged.

Yehti shuddered, and with an unearthly wail, began to sob and sob and sob. Huge, globulous, light blue tears streamed from its eye into the sponge. Uta patted Yehti.

"There, there, my love. It's all right. Let out your sorrow."

"Uta!" called Imogen. "We caught them! We caught the twins!"

Uta Glögg sprang to her feet and clapped her hands.

"Excellent! Most excellent! Away with them now!"

"How shall we kill them, Uta?" asked Imogen.

"So many ways, so many ways," said Uta Glögg. "Should they burn, should we sting, should we slice, should they swing?"

"I've always enjoyed a good 'And they plunged to their deaths' scenario," said a voice the twins recognized at once. Stephanie Knightleigh stepped from a dark recess in the cave wall.

"Rrrmm mmhph," Ellen grunted. Stephanie smirked and yanked off the gag.

"You were saying?"

"Stephanie," said Ellen. "I knew you were behind all this."

"No, no," said Stephanie, nodding curtly at Uta Glögg. "I am merely an extra pair of hands."

"I like plunging deaths," chortled Uta. "We will throw them into the mine!"

"The abandoned diamond mine," said Stephanie. "Perfect. Even if they do survive the fall, they won't survive the mine moths."

"Mine moths! Mine moths!" cackled Uta Glögg, clapping happily. *"Pretty wings and shiny jaws!"*

"Wait! Wait!" shouted Ellen as Gonzalo hoisted her and Edgar over his shoulder. The rest of the conspirators followed him toward the cave entrance.

"The trap!" mouthed Edgar. "We'll be the first ones into it!"

But just feet away from the entrance Gonzalo turned and led them down a tunnel so low everyone had to duck. Slung as they were over Gonzalo's shoulder, Edgar and Ellen couldn't duck, and their bottoms bumped the sharp rocks of the ceiling.

They followed this tunnel for quite a distance, wending and weaving through the mountain. At last, they walked into daylight on the far side of the Glöggenheim.

"Multiple exits!" said Edgar. "I hadn't counted on that."

A row of mine cars sat on rusted tracks that led down into a man-made mineshaft. Imogen unhitched the lead car, and Gonzalo tossed both twins in. He reached inside and grabbed a long metal bar that extended from a slot in the floor.

"Y'all won't be needing *this*," he said, and he wrenched off the brake handle.

The twins peered over the edge of the car. Just inside the mineshaft, the tracks descended at an altogether unhealthy pitch and disappeared into darkness.

"The out-of-control mine car," said Imogen. "Now, that's a classy way to go."

"You can't throw us down there!" cried Ellen.

"Sure we can!" said Gonzalo, starting to push the car. "It's easy, see? Just one, two, thr—"

"Wait!" said Phoebe, and everyone turned.

"What's the matter?" asked Imogen.

"I just— I d-don't know," said Phoebe. "Maybe we don't have to *k-kill* them. . . ."

"Listen to that chatter. You must be *freezing*," said Stephanie. She pulled a Thermos from her coat pocket. "Here, drink this. It will warm you up."

Phoebe took the Thermos and drank obediently. Almost immediately she turned back to the twins with that eerie Heimertz smile spread across her pale cheeks.

"Oh, the diamond mines!" she said. "That's the perfect place to dump them. How clever!"

"Well," said Stephanie, "what are you waiting for? Push them in!"

"Stephanie, don't do this! You don't want our blood on your hands!" Edgar pleaded.

Stephanie patted Edgar's shoulder. "Of *course* I don't," she said. "That's why I'm wearing *gloves*."

And with that, Gonzalo shoved the car, and it and the twins plunged into the mine.

19. Mine, All Mine

"AAAAAAAAHHHHHHHHHH!" screamed the twins as the mine car flew down the steep slope. More than once they could feel the car tilt onto two wheels as it barreled around a curve.

"Edgar! How do we stop this thing?" cried Ellen.

"Go get that brake handle from Gonzalo and we'll talk," said Edgar.

The car careened around another turn, throwing the twins like a pair of dice in a tumbler.

"I can't—*ow!*—reach my knots!" shouted Ellen. "Can you?"

"Proving to be a little—*oof!*—difficult at the moment," said Edgar. He tried to sound calm, but even the clamor of the rusty, rushing wheels could not disguise the panic rising in his voice.

The cart snapped left and right, sometimes teetering on two wheels at a time, and the twins bounced about even harder. Untying knots backward in the dark might have been a trifle for the twins under normal circumstances, but while tumbling to and fro in a careening mine cart, the task was nigh impossible.

Impossible and hopeless.

And then a faint yellow light appeared in the air, floating above their heads. Edgar had heard stories of near-death experiences, and surely this was one: A small point of light had opened above them, and soon, he thought, it would blossom into a glowing tunnel of golden luminosity that would lead them to the afterlife.

"Head into the light, Ellen," said Edgar. "Our time is nigh. . . ."

"What? Edgar that's no light—that's Pet!"

It was true. The yellow glow came from Pet's faintly luminescent eye peering at them from over the edge of the car.

"We have a stowaway!" cried Ellen. "Pet, you brilliant mop!"

"Untie my knots, Pet, quickly!" demanded Edgar. "We haven't got much— Hey!"

Something heavy hit Edgar on the head, smashing his face to the metal floor of the mine car. Edgar smelled the distinct odors of pine tar, axle grease, mildew, and aged leather. He knew at once this was his own satchel that Pet had flung on top of him. Pet hopped into the open bag and began rummaging through. It pulled out Edgar's headlamp and turned it on: The walls of rock rushed past them at a dizzying pace.

"Oh . . . we're going really . . . really fast," Ellen whispered. The wheels screamed louder and the rock whizzed past; they had begun to pick up speed.

"Pet?" said Edgar. "The knots?"

Pet held the headlamp up and examined Gonzalo's knot. The little creature scratched its eyeball with a lone tendril and gave a little shrug.

"Escape proof and *Pet proof?*" moaned Ellen. "Oh, this just keeps getting better."

"Wait!" said Edgar. "I have an idea! Pet, look in the satchel for a pipe wrench, a screwdriver . . . anything with a handle!"

Pet rifled through the satchel. It tossed aside many wires, wing nuts, and beakers, but no handled tool.

The rock walls disappeared, and the sound of the screeching mine car changed: They had left the narrow tunnel and entered a large, echoing space. Ellen peeped over the edge of the car.

"I can't see a blasted thing!" she shouted. "Wait, wait, I think there's a sign ahead."

The light of the headlamp was just strong enough to illuminate the passing wooden sign with sloppy red letters painted across its face:

BRIDGE OUT
FOR SAFETY'S SAKE, CONSIDER SLOWING DOWN!

"Aiiieee!" screamed the twins.

"Pet! The knots!" cried Ellen.

"Nuts to the knots—get the wrench!" cried Edgar.

At last Pet pulled forth the silver hammer Edgar had taken from the museum.

"That'll do! Now, Pet, the brake—"

But the creature had already caught on. It jammed the hammer into the slot where the brake handle had been, and tapped about. Gently, gently, gently it wiggled until something clicked into place. And then—

Screeeeeeeeeee!

Pet pulled on the makeshift brake handle with all its might. Edgar and Ellen slammed into the front of the car as it suddenly decelerated.

"Pull, Pet, pull!" they cried.

The sound of the rusty brakes deafened them all, and although the car still rocked and wobbled along the track, it did so with a distinctly less dangerous demeanor. Soon the car skidded to a complete stop. Not ten feet ahead of them, the tracks ended in midair. How far they would have fallen down that sickening gulf, they could not tell.

"Thank your follicles down to their greasy little roots," said Edgar.

"I'll never chase you with hair clippers again," said Ellen. "Undo these ropes and I'll cross my heart when I say that."

Pet pulled a crooked pruning saw from the satchel and went to work at Ellen's ropes. But soon the twins noticed something disturbing: They were swaying ever so slightly to and fro.

"Is the car moving again?" asked Ellen.

"Not the car—the bridge!" said Edgar. The wooden trestle beneath them groaned. "The broken bridge can't support our weight out here in the middle!"

"Can't we catch *just one break*?" screamed Ellen. She flexed against her half-sawn ropes and burst out of them.

"Cut my ropes!" Edgar pleaded.

"No time," said Ellen. "Just hold tight."

She released the makeshift brake handle with a kick as she leaped over the front edge of the car. Planting both feet on a rotting railroad tie, she leaned into the mine car with all her strength. At first, it didn't budge, but Ellen gritted her teeth and strained every muscle and sinew in her body, and slowly, the wheels began to squeak.

"I'm almost free, Ellen! I'll help!"

"No time. No time!"

The bridge wobbled and rumbled as Ellen strove to move the mine car back to solid earth. She pushed and pushed, Pet sawed and sawed, and Edgar helplessly shouted encouragement.

Somewhere far beneath Ellen's feet they heard a mighty crack, and the bridge shuddered violently. Ellen could feel the bridge beginning to give way.

With the railroad ties practically slipping away from beneath her feet as she ran, Ellen plowed forward, ignoring the crushing exhaustion in her muscles and certain death chasing her from behind.

"Almost there!" shouted Edgar, though it was too dark for him to tell whether or not he was blatantly lying.

As it turned out, Edgar's blind optimism was correct, and indeed they were practically off the bridge. Alas, practicality and reality are far, far apart, even for an optimist. Though two wheels of the mine car had crossed onto solid rock, the back two weren't when the entire trestle collapsed. The car plunged down the treacherous slope leading away from the gulf's edge.

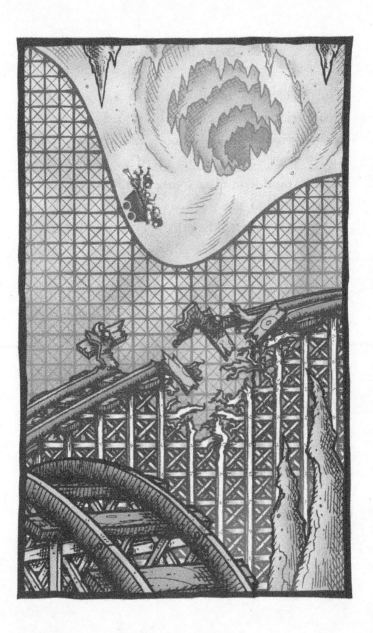

20. A Walk in the Dark

They descended into the pitch black, a wild roller-coaster ride heading ever downward. Ellen clung to the front of the car like a hood ornament, and Edgar and Pet crouched inside, terrified that the next bump would send Ellen flying off into the gloom.

At long last the slope seemed to level off, and though the cart still flew along at a clip, it had lost its terminal speed. Edgar dared to hope it would eventually roll to an uneventful stop. But then they hit a pothole, overturning the car and sending the lot of them flying. Edgar hit the rocky ground with an *ooph* and lay there for several minutes in the dark, unsure that he didn't have a bruised spleen, or at least a broken rib or two.

The headlamp was not far away from him; the bulb was turned toward the ground, and only its edges glowed against the earth. Edgar crawled to it and strapped it on. Ellen lay nearby, and Pet was farther on, shaking the dirt out of its hair.

"We must be part feline," said Ellen, rubbing her head. "Nine lives and all that."

"I wonder how many we have left after that ride," said Edgar. He helped Ellen to her feet and picked up his satchel, lying near the toppled mine car. "Come on, we've got to get out of here."

He tossed her a flashlight from his satchel.

"Can you let me rest a minute?" said Ellen. "I just saved your tail."

"And I'm most appreciative," said Edgar. "But we've got limited oxygen down here, no food, no water, and no idea how to get out. We've got to get moving."

The twins and Pet started walking, looking for any passage leading upward. It was strangely warm, and the twins sweated in their parkas. Around them, the rock glittered.

"Diamonds," said Edgar, examining the rock. "Enough to encrust our whole house."

"But why'd they stop mining, then?" asked Ellen. "It looks like there are still thousands of gems left down here."

Edgar thought for a minute.

"The volcano," he said. "That's why it's so hot down here. Maybe they dug too close to the heart of the volcano."

"Let's hope not," said Ellen. "I don't fancy actually falling out of the frying pan and into the fire."

Soon the earth sloped farther down into the

mountain, the opposite direction the twins wanted to go. But they came upon a narrow tunnel that diverged and seemed to lead up out of the mountain instead of down, so they followed it until it broke off into a thin fissure, which led to another opening above. They traveled for over an hour in this way, trying this crawl space and that passage, that hole and this gap. It was slow going, and sometimes they had to go down in order to go up, leaving them very unsure just where in the mountain they were. They sang a song to keep their spirits up on this exhausting trek:

> *Betrayed by those who once were friends,*
> *Who tried to orchestrate our ends,*
> *Our only hope now to ascend*
> *Through solid mountain crust;*
> *Swallowed by sulfuric gloom,*
> *And buried in a sweltering tomb,*
> *Left to linger in our doom*
> *And our bones turn to dust.*

"So Uta Glögg must be the person Nod warned us about," said Edgar as they hiked. "But I'll be bludgeoned if I know why *she's* calling the shots.

And what's going on with the Irregulars? They were collecting balm for Uta and Stephanie. Do you think they've betrayed the circus?"

"Not willingly," said Ellen, pulling herself up a tiny tunnel. "I think I know why they're doing these things, and why Uta was reading Yehti that sad story. She's collecting its tears and then feeding them to the Irregulars—they're hypnotized, just like I was when Pet cried into my food."

"But you weren't fully hypnotized—you weren't under anybody else's control," said Edgar. "You were just creepily well-behaved."

"I was very responsive to suggestion," said Ellen. "And that was from just one or two tears per serving. What if they're gorging the Irregulars with that evil potion? Maybe a higher dose produces a stronger effect."

"Strong enough to make people commit murder?"

"It's possible. Don't you see, Edgar? The Irregulars were perfectly nice and polite to us, right up until they tried to kill us. And remember, just before they pushed us in here, Phoebe objected."

"Oh, yeah," said Edgar. "Stephanie made her drink something."

"Exactly," said Ellen. "And it was like a switch flipped. I'm telling you, they're being hypnotized with tears and made to do whatever Uta or Stephanie wants them to."

"I could use an army of hypnotized goons to do my bidding," Edgar mused.

"We have to de-hypnotize them," Ellen continued. "We can't trap Uta and Stephanie all by ourselves."

"Especially not with Yehti on their side," said Edgar.

"Right," said Ellen. "But how? The only cure we know of for Pet tears are seeds from a *Nepenthes* plant, like Morella, and there's no way those plants could grow here in the Arctic, and I didn't bring any with me. Blast!"

"We might be out of lives, Sister."

21. Pretty Wings, Shiny Jaws

They reached a passageway that stank of sulfur. Steam poured out of a crack in the rock wall, and a red glow pulsed inside it somewhere.

"We must be really close to the volcano pit," she

said. Suddenly something whipped past her, knocking the flashlight out of her hand.

"Pet, was that you?" Ellen demanded.

"No, Pet's over here by me," said Edgar. Another *swoosh*, and Edgar's headlamp hit the ground too. The lightbulb shattered.

Suddenly a flurry of wings and fur seemed to descend on the twins and Pet.

"Aaaiiiee! Let go, let go!" wailed Edgar. Ellen finally managed to snatch up her flashlight and shined it at her brother. A bizarre creature lunged at him. It was mothlike, but as large as a poodle, with huge, silvery wings that glittered like the diamonds in the walls. It had a furry body and glassy eyes, but unlike any moth Ellen had seen before, it had two sharp fangs and they were currently digging into Edgar's big toe.

"My toe!" he screamed. "I need that for kicking my sister. Let go!"

Pet launched itself at the moth, but the beast threw the hairball against the wall with one flap of its enormous wings. Pet crumpled into a hairy heap. Ellen leaped at the moth and started beating it with her flashlight. The moth pulled its fangs from Edgar's toe and flew at Ellen, who just dodged a nasty bite. She held the moth back with her fore-arm, but the creature beat its wings with such force, it propelled her into a wall, pinning her.

Edgar clutched his throbbing toe and shouted curses as Pet roused itself and jumped on the beast's back, covering its eyes with a tangle of tendrils.

The moth reeled backward, bucking wildly and ramming itself against the walls to crush the burden on its back—but Pet held on. Ellen struggled to her feet, still clutching the flashlight. She whacked the moth again and again.

"Squash, stupid bug!" she hollered. "Squash! Squash! Squash!"

At last the creature fell lifeless to the ground. Ellen collapsed beside it, trying to catch her breath. She and Pet crawled over to Edgar. Pet wrapped itself around Edgar's toe, acting as a tourniquet, but Edgar brushed the creature away with a snarl.

"Couldn't it have bitten my arm? *That* would have left a scar to be proud of," he muttered.

22. A Mine Moth Is a Terrible Thing to Waste

"Well, we're down one light source, and we're being hunted by weird beasts," said Ellen. "I'm starting to think the mine car would have been an easier way to go."

"All is not lost," said Edgar. He shone the flashlight on his wounded footie, where Ellen could make out a silvery powder shining on it. "These nasties leave a residue. In fact, I found a trail of this stuff leading through that fissure up there."

"So?" asked Ellen.

"I think we should follow it," said Edgar. "The moth probably came from a place with air and water. The trail might lead us out of here."

"Or straight to its lair with a dozen moth mouths to feed," said Ellen.

"What do you want, an air-conditioned elevator ride?" asked Edgar. "We're lost, and we're not going to last much longer down here. Do you have a better idea?"

Neither Ellen nor Pet did, so off they went, climbing and clambering and scrambling up through the tunnels like before, only this time using the traces of silvery powder as their guide. The trail shimmered in the illumination of the flashlight. But within the hour, the light began to flicker and fade, until its beam was no brighter than Pet's own faintly glowing eyeball.

"Not yet, not yet," Edgar begged.

But the light winked out, and that was that. They were in complete darkness.

"Dratted batteries!" wailed Edgar. "Suffocated in the bowels of a mountain, left to rot, and mine moths pick our bones . . ."

"Wait!" Ellen sniffed the air. "That draft of air didn't seem quite so hot and stifling. It felt almost . . . cool . . ."

"Which way did it come from?"

"This way!" Ellen's voice was already moving away.

"Saved!" cried Edgar, crawling after it.

In the next minute, the air *did* start to feel cooler, and fresher, too. And when they felt the fissure take a distinct upward turn, they smelled something earthy and dense, a scent they knew well.

"Balm!" said Edgar.

"Shh, not so loud," said Ellen. "If we really are nearing the balm spring, we're getting closer to our enemies, too."

They saw a soft aura of light in the distance. In the unrelenting darkness it looked almost unreal, like a mirage. Edgar was the first to reach it and poke his head out of a narrow gap. He almost laughed when he saw where he was.

"Sister!" he said. "We're back in business!"

Ellen climbed up next to her brother, followed by Pet, and they saw that he was right. They had come to the cavern they had first encountered several hours before, when they'd been betrayed by the Midway Irregulars.

This time, they got a better look. The cavern was lit by an electric lamp that hung from a crooked metal hook. By the lamplight, they could tell the

EDGAR & ELLEN

cavern was about as large as Uta Glögg's den, but the ceiling was much higher, maybe twenty feet up, and it peaked in the center. The floor was just as steep as they remembered, and they had to watch their step lest they tumble downhill. If they had, they might have landed in the light blue goop of the balm spring, which bubbled at the far end of the cave.

Ellen noticed something else: greenish-blue leafy plants with bulbous heads, growing around the spring.

"*Nepenthes*, Edgar," she murmured. "Of course, the volcano makes it hot enough for them to grow. We can save the Irregulars after all."

She was about to dart down to the spring when Edgar caught her arm. Voices were coming from the tunnel leading from Uta's den, and soon Uta herself, Stephanie, and Imogen emerged, heading straight for the spring.

"When does Ginger-hair hold up her end of the bargain?" Uta asked.

"It's almost time now," Stephanie replied. "Soon you shall have every, uh, flavor of pudding. You will control it all."

"Ha ha! All the pudding in the world!" Uta laughed, dancing back and forth.

Imogen started loading up a bucket with balm. The *Nepenthes* snapped at her, but she took care to avoid their bites.

"Why don't you go and prepare Yehti?" Stephanie said to Uta Glögg. "We should be all packed and ready to go."

"Run, run! Skip, skip! Glögg is going on a trip!" Uta hooted, and she skittered merrily back up the tunnel.

"We're taking her with us, then?" said Imogen once Uta Glögg had gone.

"Of course not," said Stephanie impatiently. "I don't have to explain the plan to you *again*, do I?"

"But you just said—"

"I was *lying* to her. Geez, you all need to perfect your deception skills if you're going to continue as my henchmen."

"I'm so sorry about that, Miss Stephanie," said Imogen. "So she's going to stay here without her pet?"

Stephanie grabbed Imogen by the shoulders.

"For the last time," she said, "we're destroying this place. Preferably with Uta inside."

23. A-Goggled

"Now, are you finished loading the stuff?" asked Stephanie, glancing at the bucket full of balm that Imogen carried.

"All set," she replied.

"Then it's time to go. We should have enough collected from here."

She and Imogen started back up the path, treading close by the twins. Stephanie paused and sniffed the air.

"What is it?" asked Imogen. Stephanie shook her head.

"Nothing," she said as they withdrew. "I thought I smelled something."

Edgar and Ellen scrambled out of the narrow fissure and into the cavern. "We haven't got much time," he said. "Pet and I will follow Stephanie. We have the element of surprise; maybe we can get the jump on her."

"And if Yehti gets the jump on *you*?" asked Ellen.

"Pet and I scramble. Somewhere in this maze of tunnels is the way out. We'll lead it up to the trap," said Edgar. He picked up the electric lamp and handed it to Ellen. "You stay down here and collect the seeds, then try to feed them to the Irregulars."

"How am I supposed to do that?" asked Ellen. "Ring the dinner bell?"

"I dunno—a canapé? You'll think of something," said Edgar, and he and Pet disappeared up the tunnel after Stephanie and Imogen.

"A canapé," she muttered. "What a comedian."

Holding the electric lamp in front of her, she stepped cautiously down the cavern and approached the spring. A healthy patch of plants grew off to one side, and they curled menacingly when Ellen approached with the light.

But then she heard some scuffling off in the distance, and she snapped off the lantern. Footsteps fumbled into the room, and she heard the sound of hands swishing over the walls and floor as if looking for something in the dark.

"That's odd," said Imogen. "I was sure I left that lantern in here."

Imogen shuffled closer. Ellen could hear her sweeping her foot left and right, looking for the lantern. Ellen knew that in a few moments, Imogen would stumble upon her, and she drew as close as she dared to the *Nepenthes* patch. Any nearer and she would probably be within snapping range of the plants' teeth. Still, she nudged closer, and she heard a faint *hiss* and *snap* near her ear.

"Uh-oh," said Imogen. "Not today, you little beasts. Miss Stephanie says not to get near you, and she never steers us wrong!"

Imogen made her way back up the tunnel, tutting to herself about losing her lantern.

"That was close, friends. Thanks," said Ellen and she snapped the light back on. Then she got a good look at the plants that were straining their stems to bite her. She gasped.

"You're not *Nepenthes sinestros* at all!" she said. "I've never *seen* a species like you."

It was true. Though these plants had the same pitcher-shaped gullet and seed-lined jaws of Morella, her beloved *Nepenthes sinestros*, they had a number of distinct differences.

"Varegated petals? Oversize operculum? Ridged peristome? You're beautiful!" Ellen enthused. "You're a new species, and you need a new name. How about *Nepenthes arcticus*?"

She tugged a pigtail as she watched her new friends lunge at her. Their jaws snapped at the air.

"Lovely," said Ellen, and she patted one on the

head. It nearly snagged her finger. "Time to harvest some of your seeds, my beauties."

But then she heard a sound from the tunnel that led from Uta's den. Someone was coming back.

Ellen acted fast. If *Nepenthes arcticus* was anything like her beloved *sinestros*, it would shed its seeds from its mouth every night; if so, there would be plenty to harvest tucked beneath those variegated fronds. She slipped her hand beneath the leaves and, sure enough, found some seeds—but she could grab only one before the jaws of the plants struck.

"That will have to do," she whispered, and she turned off the light. Then she crept up the steep incline to return the lantern where Imogen could find it.

She hung the lantern back on the hook and listened at the mouth of the tunnel, but heard no other sounds. After several minutes in the silent dark, Ellen began her climb up the tunnel. That's when she felt someone grab her wrist.

"Not again," she muttered.

"Howdy, Miss Ellen," said Gonzalo. Someone behind him snapped the switch of a powerful lantern, and the cave flooded with bright white light.

"Augh!" Ellen clamped a hand over her eyes. The only thing she had seen amid the blazing light was a fuzzy image of Gonzalo wearing mountain climber's sun goggles that protected his eyes from the burst of light.

"Neat trick, not dying in the mine," said Imogen. "I wish you were going to live long enough to show us how you did it!"

"No problem," said Ellen. With her eyes still closed, she grabbed the goggles off Gonzalo's face.

"Yeeeehowch!" he shrieked, and let go of her wrist. Ellen dropped to a crouch and swept her leg toward the sound of the scream. She connected with Gonzalo's knees and the cowboy fell.

In the moments of confusion that followed, Ellen pulled Gonzalo's goggles over her own eyes. Properly shielded from the light, she could make out the rest of the Midway Irregulars, each wearing a pair of similar shades. Gonzalo's crumpled body had rolled downhill after he fell, knocking Imogen and Phoebe over.

Mab and Merrick, in their striped acrobatic tights, leaped gracefully over the cowboy and sprang toward Ellen with a net spread between them. Ellen barreled into the mesh of ropes with such force it jerked Mab and Merrick backward off their feet. She pulled the two circus acrobats for several yards before her feet became entangled in the net. She fell as Imogen charged her.

"Orders are orders, Ellen," she said through an unnaturally wide smile. "Sorry!"

"Not sorry enough," growled Ellen, untangling herself. She flung the net at Imogen.

The future ringmaster dodged it easily, but it gave Ellen all the time she needed. She leaped forward and planted her head squarely in Imogen's gut.

"Oof!" Imogen tumbled toward the balm

spring—a familiar *crunch* and Imogen's "Yow!" told Ellen that the *Nepenthes arcticus* had at last found something to bite.

That left little Phoebe, wide-eyed and worried.

"You're finished, Phoebe!" said Ellen, but her boast was a bluff: She wanted Mab and Merrick to think she had forgotten them. But, oh, she had not.

Just as the acrobats jumped at her from behind, Ellen dropped to all fours. Mab and Merrick overshot their target and landed in a pile in front of her.

"Ho, ho!" Ellen shouted in triumph. "*I'm* the striped champion around here!"

Ellen leaped and brought down a footie onto each of their rumps.

"Ha! That leaves only helpless little—"

WHUMP!

Phoebe charged Ellen, knocking her into a wall. The little seed in Ellen's hand fell loose as she felt the wind knocked out of her. Before Ellen could recover, Phoebe tossed Gonzalo's lasso over Ellen's head and cinched her elbows to her sides.

"I never could lasso moving targets," said Phoebe. "Thanks for holding still."

24. Do Kitties Go to Heaven?

After taking a few wrong turns in the labyrinthine tunnels and bumping into some dead ends, Edgar and Pet followed the scent of Uta Glögg's fetid lair to their target. They tiptoed close to an opening that gave them a clear look inside the old woman's den. Stephanie was speaking to Uta in the smaller room off to the side, where the twins had seen the hag reading to Yehti.

". . . a little suspicious," said Stephanie softly. Edgar couldn't quite make it out. ". . . sent the whole team just in case . . . can't be too cautious . . . harder to kill than slipgibbet weed . . ."

"I hope she's not on to us," whispered Edgar to Pet. "Let's hurry."

There was no trace of the monster. Edgar and Pet ran noiselessly to the cave entrance, and for the first time in hours, Edgar felt cold, fresh air on his face. Despite the frigid temperatures, it was a welcome sensation.

He and Pet got to work, checking the tension on the cables that held the bell, which still swayed above the cave entrance. The tripwires seemed in good shape, and the pitons were holding steady, but for the first time he realized how slapdash their construction had been. It was hastily assembled and untested, and in all probability would horribly backfire.

"Looks complicated," said a voice behind him.

Before he could look up, Stephanie had leaped upon him. She lodged her knee in Edgar's back, squeezing the air out of him like toothpaste from a tube. He squirmed and wriggled and bucked, but Stephanie held firm.

"Uta? I have him for you!"

"Ginger has a surprise for us!" Uta's voice bubbled with glee. "Shall we open the present, Yehti? See what's inside?"

Though most of his face was smushed into the mountainside, Edgar could see the old woman's gnarled, bare feet step beside his head. Yehti emerged from behind a rock; the creature was harnessed to a large sleigh laden with crates. Edgar could guess what they contained.

"Slippery, sneaky, shoes are leaky," cackled Uta. "Naughty boy cheats his death; eat him raw, smell my breath."

"Lady, you are nuttier than almond bark," said Edgar.

"And you are dead," said Uta curtly, and Edgar felt a thick braid of Yehti's hair wrap around his neck and lift him high. He struggled to breathe. Uta clapped her hands as the monster's tendrils tightened.

As stars began to dance before his eyes, Edgar caught sight of Pet also entangled tight in Yehti's hairy grip. Pet was buried so deep, it couldn't so much as wave good-bye. A single tear dripped from its eye.

And Edgar had an idea.

"Yehti, what about little Winky, Trinky, and uh, Mop?" he asked. "Remember the little kitties who couldn't survive the river? Their story has a sequel: The little kitties couldn't find kitty heaven!"

Yehti's grip loosened. The pupil of its eye grew big, and the great orb swelled with moisture.

"That's right, Yehti, these little kitties got *super* lost, because Kinky had misplaced his glasses. He couldn't see! And . . . Inky was deaf, so she couldn't hear the angels calling . . . and Flop never learned to read, so he couldn't follow the signs. They were lost for eternity!"

Yehti's body shivered, and a drop the size of a water balloon fell from its eye.

"For crying out loud—the kitties aren't real!" cried Stephanie. "They were never even alive in the first place!"

At this, Yehti cried even harder.

"Bwaaaaaaa!" it howled.

Uta took a stick and poked the beast, but this only made the monster sadder. It slumped to the ground, disconsolate. Edgar felt himself slipping loose—but before he could, Stephanie seized him in a choke hold. Edgar reached for a hunk of red hair, but Uta stepped on his knuckles.

A flash of dark hair whizzed in front of him. He looked up to see that Pet had glommed onto Stephanie's face and was gripping her entire head in its tresses.

"My nose! My nose!" Stephanie screeched. "Get your nasty, greasy hairs out of my nose!" She let go of Edgar to pry Pet off her face. "Yuck! Yuck!"

She tossed the creature aside and anxiously wiped strands of hair from her nose and mouth.

Wielding a needle-sharp icicle, Uta dove upon him next. The weapon gleamed cold and deadly as she thrust it toward Edgar.

Ptang!

A rock ricocheted off Uta's back, and she staggered. She grimaced as a torrent of stones, ice hunks, and well-compacted snowballs followed the first volley.

Ptang! Pthunk! Ptonk!

It was Pet, spinning like a roulette wheel and flinging anything it could get its tendrils on. Its aim was inexact, but the hail of pesky snowballs gave Uta fits until she dropped her icicle spear.

Edgar saw his chance. With a quick glance at the bell to confirm his calculations, he leaped to his feet, pushed Uta into Stephanie, and shoved both of them into the lap of the sobbing snow monster.

He wrapped thick cords of Yehti's hair around the two of them and (while dodging swipes of Uta's talonlike hands) tied them snug in a swift Three-Fingered Violinist's knot.

He dashed to the tripwire that stretched across the mouth of the cave. With a kick of his foot, the wire *spronged* loose, and Edgar ducked out of the way to let the diamond bell fall on the perfectly situated trio.

Nothing happened.

"No, no, no!" he cried. "They're exactly where they need to be! Fall, trap, fall!"

He scrambled atop the cave to the fulcrum that held the bell in place. The diamond bell swayed in the cold breeze, but its support rope held tight.

"It's stuck!" called Edgar to Pet below. "I need something to knock it loose."

Pet scurried into Edgar's satchel and tossed aside the first few implements its little hairs came across: a windshield wiper blade, a length of garden hose, a lump of putty that possibly could have been a sandwich once. Then it surfaced with the antique silver hammer.

Pet chucked the hammer as hard as it could at Edgar. The throw was strong, if a little too high.

As Edgar saw that shimmering silver hammer flying end over end, he realized with sudden, startling certainty: This was no hammer at all, but the very clapper that had rung the bell on the day of the Breaking. It was obvious to him now. And it was sailing in a beautiful arc toward its old foe, the diamond bell.

25. Lord of the Ring

Edgar sprang for the clapper, reaching as high as he could. He felt instant relief as his fingers wrapped around it just before it hit the bell.

"Whew," he gasped. "That was close."

Stephanie tackled him from behind. Her wrists trailed knotted threads of white hair she had yanked out while escaping Yehti's mane. She wrenched the silver clapper from Edgar's hand.

"Not close enough," she said, and she swung the clapper with all her might.

DINNNNNNNNNNNGGGGGG

As perky Lilja had promised, it was the purest tone Edgar had ever heard, a resonance of raw, primal sound, and it wouldn't stop ringing in his ears.

NNNNNNGGGGG

If possible, it seemed to get louder as it reverberated, until he wasn't even sure if it was the bell
ringing or the inside of his skull.

NNNNNNGGGGG

Edgar glanced down at his hands, which were flat
upon the ground and suddenly tingly. His knuckles
were blurry. At first he thought it was a problem
with his eyesight, then he realized the snow, the
mountain—everything was trembling.

NNNNNNGGGGG

"The Breaking!" cried Uta. "Not again. Not
here. Not so close! It will end all!" Then her cry
redoubled. "*My pudding!* Not a drop to be lost, not
a drop!"

Uta wriggled out of her binds and staggered
toward the cave entrance. The mountain was moving beneath them and even Edgar, crouching on
hands and knees, found it hard to keep his bal-
ance. Yehti tried to follow Uta, but the shaking
finally loosened the stubborn trap cable and the
bell dropped on top of the beast. The giant mound
of white fur disappeared under the dome and the
incessant reverberation stopped.

But the damage had been done. A loud, echoing

crack and a *whoosh* from far up the slope told them
that an avalanche had been set loose—but consider-
ing the cracks splitting the ground beneath them, it
was probably the least of their worries.

Uta did not stop to contemplate any of this, however. She plunged into the cave just as the rocks
around the mouth succumbed to the shaking and
collapsed. Yehti threw off its diamond cage and bellowed after its master, but the rocks continued to
crumble and sink, as if the entire cave were melting
like so much candle wax.

Stephanie climbed into the sleigh, grabbed
the reins, and whipped them across Yehti's back.
It reared and charged down the mountain with
so much force that it threw Stephanie out of the
driver's seat. She hung onto the reins for a few feet,
dragging behind, but after a hard knock against a
rock, she let go.

"No! Wait! Come back," Stephanie cried, but
her escape vehicle was already disappearing down
the mountainside.

Edgar looked up and saw a rushing wall of snow
bearing down on them.

"We've got to get out of—" he started to yell,
but then the world exploded.

26. Boiling Over

DINNNNNNNNNGGGGGGGG

In the lantern-lit cavern, the sound of the chiming bell echoed and echoed, boring into Ellen's ears. It rattled her teeth and shivered in her bones, until she realized it wasn't just the bell reverberating, but the mountain itself. Phoebe fell and let go of Ellen, but in a moment they were both rolling down the steep tunnel. Phoebe tried to cry out to the rest of the Midway Irregulars, but the rumbling ground was too loud.

Ellen tumbled to avoid the bite of a *Nepenthes*. As she did so, a chunk of floor fell away right next to her, leaving a gaping hole. Heat radiated up through it, and when Ellen looked in, she could see the swirling, boiling magma of the volcano far below. Ellen shrugged off the lasso and tried to stagger toward the exit, but the ground ahead of her broke apart. As she and the Irregulars watched helplessly, their only means of escape crumbled and plummeted into the magma.

"What do we do?" cried Mab.

"We're goners for sure!" said Merrick.

The heat was turning the chamber into a kiln.

If they didn't find a way out soon, they'd cook like turkeys—if they didn't fall into the magma first.

Then Ellen saw something that made her stomach flip-flop. In all the commotion, they had forgotten about the balm—the very combustible, very explosive balm. The ground around the spring fell away before Ellen's eyes and dropped into the widening fissure. The mouth of the bubbling spring began to follow; streams of steaming blue balm trickled down toward the magma.

"Get the balm!" Ellen shouted at the Irregulars.

"Oh, we've already harvested enough," Imogen shouted back. "Thanks for checking!"

"No, you don't understand!" Ellen cried. "The balm will explo—"

Just then, the first drops of balm hit the magma pit.

"Take cover!" screamed Ellen, but her words were drowned by explosions that shook the cavern even more violently, as the dripping balm hit the magma and ignited. A

gap opened between Ellen and the Irregulars, and she found herself stranded on an island of rock.

A jet of steam blew a hole through the top of the cave. Ellen ducked as pieces of the ceiling fell around her, but she felt something else, too: cold, fresh air. Clouds passed overhead, visible through the hole that had just opened. Escape!

"Gotta climb like I've never climbed before," she said.

The Midway Irregulars were thinking the same thing. Gonzalo gathered his lasso and tossed it through the opening, but it caught only air and fell back down. Again and again he tried, until at last the rope caught an outcropping of rock. One by one the Irregulars scurried up. Imogen was last, and

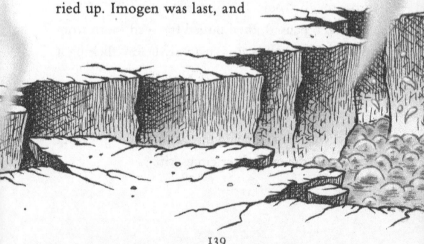

as she gained the top, she looked back down at Ellen.

"Throw me the rope!" Ellen called up. Imogen looked as if she were contemplating it—but then she shook her head.

"You still have to die!" she shouted back. "I—I'm not sure why, but I know—I know you're supposed to die."

"You don't have to do this, Imogen! You've been hypnotized," called Ellen. Then she saw a bleeding wound on Imogen's arm with what looked like a tooth protruding from it—her tumble through the *Nepenthes arcticus* patch had obviously ended with a nasty bite. "The antidote! It's breaking the spell, Imogen. Fight it!"

"Antidote?" Imogen looked at the wound. "Hypnotized?"

"Yes, yes! Stephanie's been poisoning you. Now throw me the rope. Throw me the rope!"

Imogen paused, then pulled the seed tooth from her arm. She looked at it curiously before flicking it into the magma.

"That's better," she said. "Have a super death, Ellie!"

And with that, she fled up the rope, disappearing along with the rest of her circus kin.

Now there was no hope left. Ellen could not leap, nor climb, nor tumble to safety. She was alone on her island of rock, and even that was beginning to fall apart. Panic rose in her like the smoke from the magma pit. Was this really how she was going to die?

"My pudding!" shouted a voice, and Ellen saw Uta Glögg squeeze through a crevice mere yards away. The mountain quakes had sealed off one exit from the cavern, but in the process had seemingly opened another. If Uta Glögg could get in, Ellen could get out.

"Uta!" Ellen cried. "The whole mountain is going to blow! Quick, go back! Move it!"

Ellen raced up to the old woman and tried to push her back through the crevice, but Uta Glögg grabbed both of Ellen's wrists. Despite the urgency, Ellen could not help but marvel at the crone's wiry strength.

"What have you done to the pudding?" Uta screamed in Ellen's face. Ellen felt nauseated at her rancid breath. Mixed with the volcano's sulfuric fumes swirling around them, Ellen was sure she would pass out if she didn't breathe clean air soon.

"Let me go, you old hag!" she shouted back at Uta Glögg, wrenching herself free. "We're both going to die down here if we don't go now!"

She tried to push past Uta and through the crevice. But at that moment, a colossal tremor shook the cavern, and the ground beneath Ellen's and Uta's feet fell away, taking both of them with it.

27. To Have and to Hold On

Ellen reached out for anything that would stop her freefall. For a few eternal seconds there was nothing to grab. And then, miraculously, her fingers closed around something sturdy, and her body bashed against the scalding rock wall. She held on, dangling precariously from the cliff face, and peered up to see what had saved her.

She had grasped the stem of a *Nepenthes arcticus*, a sturdy specimen from the looks of it. The stem was thick as tree roots, and it held fast. Ellen's eyes burned, and she could barely breathe from the smoke and ash, but at least she wasn't high-diving into a volcano.

She felt a tug on her footies; Uta Glögg had caught her ankles, and was now trying to climb up Ellen to safety.

"You're going to bring us both down!" Ellen

shouted, but Uta Glögg took no notice. She thrashed about, clinging desperately to Ellen's legs, and Ellen struggled to maintain her grip on the stem. Something stabbed Ellen's hand, and she looked up to see the *Nepenthes* biting her fingers.

"Ow!" Ellen yelled, though she knew the plant was just trying to protect itself. The pain was incredible. She couldn't hang on much longer.

"*PUDDING!*" cried Uta Glögg. The melting balm spring no longer drained in trickles but in a torrent. In moments it would hit the magma, and the explosion would probably incinerate them both.

"Uta, don't!" said Ellen, but it was too late. Uta Glögg, feverish with desire for the substance, pushed off from the rock and swung like Tarzan on a vine. With amazing agility, she leaped off to grab at the oozing balm with both hands. She hit the slope and tried scooping the goop into her arms. But just as the balm was falling down the slope, so was she, and with an armload of blue goo clutched to her chest, Uta Glögg tumbled toward the roiling magma.

"I've got you, pudding, I've got you!" she cried, and Ellen averted her eyes as the old woman plunged to her death. A balm-powered explosion sent globs of magma and shards of rock shooting past Ellen's

dangling body, and she knew that the story of Uta Glögg was over.

Ellen had no time to think. The *Nepenthes* still bit her hand; with all the strength left in her, Ellen hauled herself onto the slim ridge on which the plant grew. There she collapsed, figuring death by smoke inhalation was preferable to a magma bath.

More balm spilled into the magma, and more explosions shook the cavern. Ellen closed her eyes, ready for the end. But instead, she felt cold air again on her face, and with effort, she opened her eyes.

The blast had opened another crevice. It was narrow, and Ellen could not tell how far it stretched; it could perhaps end only yards away, or another shake could close it in entirely with her inside—but the fresh air blowing through it was unmistakable, as was her desire to breathe it.

"Nothing for it," she murmured to herself, and she dragged her aching body into the pitch-black gap. It was so narrow, she had to pull herself blindly along, inch by inch.

Suddenly she heard something scritching and scratching up ahead as the tunnel began to widen. Something passed over her head. A fuzzy wing brushed her cheek.

"Mine moths!" she gasped, and without thinking, she grabbed out, catching one by its midsection. The moth bucked for an instant, and Ellen expected to feel the bite of its jaws. But its fear of the magma was greater than its annoyance with Ellen, so it plunged on, half flying, half crawling down the tunnel, dragging Ellen along with it.

"I never thought I'd be thankful for you fiends," Ellen said, hoping that this monster would lead her to safety.

28. Lovely Weather for a Sleigh Ride Together

The snow surged over them, and Edgar saw his world fill with white. Before he could be completely engulfed, he had one last desperate idea. The overturned bell was cresting this tidal wave of snow right beside him; he dove toward it. With one hand he clutched Pet and with the other he pawed at the snow like a one-handed swimmer crossing the English Channel in a hurricane.

He caught the lip of the bell and pulled himself into safety inside. The snow poured past the opening, but a pocket of air remained inside the bell.

He gave Pet a tug—it was harder than he expected to pull the creature after him, but with a mighty heave, Pet popped inside the bell . . . as did a person who was clinging to Pet's tendrils.

"Stephanie!" Edgar yelled. Or rather, he tried to yell—the bell was now flipping end over end, and his shout came out sounding more like "Splarrrg!"

Edgar, Stephanie, and Pet were a tangle of arms, legs, and hair as the bell tumbled down the mountain. None of them could tell what was up, what was down, or whether the plummet would ever stop. Edgar felt his head crack against the diamond so many times, he was starting to doubt that the hardest substance on Earth would survive against his thick skull.

Finally the tumbling slowed to a brisk roll, and a few seconds after that, a sweet, full stop. Edgar opened his eyes. Stephanie's elbow dug into his chin.

"Get off," he said, pushing her arm away.

"I think I'm broken," moaned Stephanie, sitting up and rubbing her head.

Pet's pupil seemed to bobble around in its eye before finally focusing on Edgar. It shook itself and gave a weak "tendrils-up."

They looked around, but could see nothing except white above, below, and everywhere in between. A wall of snow sealed the open end of the bell. But they were alive, for the time being, anyway.

"I am invincible!" cried Edgar, raising his fists in the air and accidentally cracking them against the top of the bell. "Ow."

"Every idiot who says that usually ends up dying five minutes later," Stephanie retorted. "Like we will if we don't get out of here. Start digging."

She and Edgar began shoveling their way to the

surface. After several minutes, teeth chattering and hands burning with cold, Edgar pulled back to rub his freezing fingers.

"Oh, no you don't," said Stephanie. "Your ugly face is *not* going to be the last thing I see on this Earth." And she heaved a pile of snow behind her.

"It's not going to help if my fingers fall off from frostbite," said Edgar. "Besides, you're not the boss here. And as I recall, it wasn't too long ago that you *wanted* me dead."

"Yes, but not if I have to join you! I—ugh, get your mutant hamster off me!" Stephanie shouted, for Pet had lunged at her and put a tendril to her lips. She flung it at Edgar, but Pet hopped back up and waved to the both of them.

"Hush! I think Pet's trying to tell us to be quiet," Edgar said. "What is it, Pet?"

Pet cupped its hair around Edgar's ear, motioning for him to listen.

"What is it?" Stephanie demanded.

"Shh! Listen," he said. "I hear voices!"

Indeed, faint voices came from somewhere above. Edgar and Stephanie shouted as loud as they could.

"Here! Here! We're in here!" they yelled, digging furiously. "Get us out!"

A hand popped through the snow and grabbed Edgar's hair.

"Found something! I think it's children!" a voice shouted, and moments later, more hands appeared, clearing away the snow and ice. They pulled Edgar, Stephanie, and Pet from the avalanche and wrapped them in blankets. Edgar saw that the bell had landed right at the edge of the ice wall. Behind them, the mountain rumbled and smoked, warning the town that the worst was far from over.

"Good goldmines, how did you two end up down here?" asked Knute.

"Our bell!" cried Big Wiigie, who had continued digging into the snow and found the giant diamond.

"Oh, right, just borrowing—" began Edgar.

"It's back, it's back!" sang the assembled citizens. "*Oofdooloolly*, they found our bell!"

Lilja herself threw her arms around Edgar. "You might just make Employee of the Month!"

"Er, yes," said Edgar. "Just stumbled across this thing and, uh, thought I'd bring it back for you."

Gürlf clapped Edgar on the back. "No hard feelings," he said. "Not for the hero of Frøsthaven!"

As Edgar shook his head at the gullibility of the

people around him, he spotted Stephanie trying to sneak away amid the hubbub.

"Not so fast, snow bunny," said Edgar, grabbing her elbow. "You're going to tell me everything I want to know about—"

Edgar's demands were cut short by a blast from the mountain.

KKKRRROOOMMM!

Snorgpeke—all of it, not just part, but every rock and pebble and splinter of wood on the whole mountain—launched skyward under a fire-engine-red stream of lava. The volcano had blown.

29. Art Criticism

The sight would have been beautiful, had it not been so terrible.

The lava plumed and coiled upward, like one of Ellen's cultivated vines, lifting the entire mass of Snorgpeke with it. Whereas most erupting volcanoes blew apart, sending smoke and ash over the surrounding landscape, Snorgpeke simply lifted skyward, like a levitating wedding cake. Perhaps it was because the mountain was so sturdy, or perhaps it was because of the way the veins of balm ignited, or perhaps it was even because this was Nature's way of granting a death befitting the Zeus of mountains.

Snorgpeke rose above them all like a small moon and, having crested so high it seemed to be in orbit, came plummeting back down, striking the ground with a force that lifted everyone in town ten feet into the air.

Snorgpeke punched through the earth's crust, leaving a valley where, a moment ago, a mountain had been.

"Sister," whispered Edgar. He stumbled and let go of Stephanie's elbow. Pet covered its eye.

The sky filled with debris and globs of lava spattered from the impact. The citizens screamed and stumbled over themselves, running for the shelter of their homes, as if a house made of ice could be much barrier to red-hot lava. But Edgar stood dumbfounded, almost forgetting the danger he was in.

"Ellen," he murmured as burning rock landed all around him. But then he saw something that defied all logic. A cluster of mine moths skimmed the meadow, and it looked like one of them was dragging a human. A human wearing stripes.

As they neared the Great Ice Wall, Ellen let go and hit the ground, tumbling until she came to a full stop before her brother. He took her hand and helped her to her feet as Pet leaped to her shoulder for a hairy hug.

"Clever," Edgar said.

"No, *lucky*," Ellen replied.

Flaming lava balls and jagged rocks showered down around them, and they raced to follow the rest of the townspeople into Frøsthaven.

With Edgar half dragging Ellen, the twins and Pet crawled under the nearest cover they could find, a bus-stop bench. This being Frøsthaven, of course, it was made of ice, and one splash of lava melted the thing right over their heads. They staggered blindly as stones and dollops of lava peppered the ground around them; they skittered through a park and dove into a gazebo, but this too took a hit from the lava and disappeared into hissing steam.

When the hailstorm of hot debris finally abated, the twins looked out from beneath the toppled snowman under which they had last taken refuge. The snowman's top hat was burned through, and its carrot nose was nicely steamed, but they had escaped intact.

"Look at the town," Edgar murmured. Ellen cleared the soot from her eyes and followed her brother's gaze. The once glittering perfection of Frøsthaven had become a twisted dream. Where shimmering spires had pierced the sky, there were now stumps resembling melted candles; the vaulted domes and regal towers that once reflected the Arctic sun into colorful prisms were lopsided and holey, as if a giant hairdryer had blown willy-nilly through town. Drops of water cascaded in rivulets down melted walls and crooked roofs, refreezing in asymmetrical, grotesque shapes. The ice wall that had protected Frøsthaven from the mountain lay in ruins.

The Frøsthaveners stumbled from their hiding places and stared in shock. In the fiery aftermath, silence hung over the entire town.

To the north, the profile of Snorgpeke no longer loomed over it all—in its place was a lingering cloud of dust and ash. Snorgpeke Mountain was now Snorgpeke Crater, where snow melted into bubbling pools of water between mounds of crumbled stone. At the very least, the falling mountain had plugged the volcano—there wasn't an ounce of lava flowing anywhere to be seen—but the once glorious peak was now only blackened wasteland at the town's doorstep.

"We've done it this time," whispered Edgar.

"They're going to lock us away forever," said Ellen.

"Well, maybe not," said Edgar. "At the moment, they think I *returned* the bell after it had been stolen. They were celebrating before the volcano popped. If we can keep quiet, maybe we can still escape."

"What saps," marveled Ellen. "What else would they be willing to believe?"

"Citizens of Frøsthaven!" called a voice through a megaphone. It was Nils deGroot standing at the foot of the (mostly melted) bell tower. "Citizens, hear me! As you look about you and consider the impact this cataclysm has had upon this town, I want to make one thing perfectly clear."

Nora deGroot pulled the megaphone away from her husband and shouted, "It's wonderful!"

The townsfolk looked at each other in confusion.

"My wife is right," said Nils deGroot. "The melted mayhem around you is an absolute *masterpiece*! An architectural treasure of nature's making! Consider the form—so free and unfettered. The randomness of the devastation—so terrible and beautiful. There's nothing else like it on Earth!"

"*Snoog!* It's true!" shouted Big Wiigie. "Hognorsk has nothing like it! Heck, Hognorsk is going to try to *copy* it."

One citizen after another nodded in agreement.

"It *is* rather breathtaking,"

"Big Wiigie is right—this will *really* set us apart!"

"Of course I'm right!" bellowed Big Wiigie. "Look at that big, beautiful crater full of steaming pools of melted ice. People the world over will line up to enjoy the health benefits of an authentic volcano hot spring! For *cloopen* out loud, we're going to attract even *more* tourists than before!"

Ellen sighed. "I guess no one's going to be blaming us for this."

"Looks like it," said Edgar, brushing slush out of Pet's hair. "Besides, it wasn't even my fault. It was Stephanie—"

"She survived?" asked Ellen. "Where? Where is she?"

"I had her . . ." Edgar's voice trailed off. "And then I lost her."

"Great, Edgar. So you blow up a mountain *and*

fail in your one teensy mission to capture Stephanie and the Yehti."

"The hail of lava distracted me a little, okay? How'd you do?"

Ellen held out her hand. Several *Nepenthes* seeds were lodged in it.

"I did okay," she said. "Come on, let's split up. Stephanie can't be far."

30. To Pledge a Dredge

But a search of the town failed to turn up the least sign of Stephanie or the Midway Irregulars. By then, the twins' eyelids drooped as low as the sun across the far horizon, and they had to admit they didn't have the strength to face Stephanie, even if they could have found her. So Edgar and Ellen limped back to the Two Seasons Hotel to catch some much-needed rest. Their room had melted into two of its neighbors, and sunk down three flights of stairs, but the beds were still soft and warm.

Morning—or, as it was in Frøsthaven, that time of day distinguished by the 7:00 hour on a clock, not by an actual sunrise—came quickly, but the twins slept on. The sun was quite high in the sky before they awoke to Pet bouncing from bed to bed to wake them up.

"Criminy, Pet, I was just dreaming of a steamy tropical island," muttered Edgar. "Did you have to bring me back to this frozen wasteland so soon?"

But Pet continued to pester them, and at last Edgar and Ellen threw off their covers. Pet waved its tendrils for the twins to follow.

"Okay, okay," said Ellen. "This had better be good."

Pet bounded through the newly transformed town. Edgar and Ellen saw the citizens cheerily going about their lives as if nothing had changed. (Though they did see one travel agency raising a new banner that read: NEW! CRATER TOURS AND HOT BATH HOLIDAYS!)

At last Pet led them to the very outskirts south of town. It pointed at a pair of sleigh tracks that led away from town.

"Thanks for nothing, Pet," said Ellen. "Those could be *anyone's* tracks."

"Hmm. Those aren't reindeer tracks," said Edgar as he carefully studied deep swish marks in the snow. "You know, Yehti was harnessed to a sleigh the last time I saw it. This could be its trail."

"Look, there are a lot of footprints where people boarded the sleigh," said Ellen. "At least six people, and . . . Aha! *Cowboy boots!*"

"So! Stephanie and the Irregulars got away in a one-beast open sleigh," said Edgar.

"I can't believe Stephanie would use that homicidal monster as transportation," said Ellen.

"I guess Yehti is still valuable to her," said Edgar. "She needs its tears to keep the Irregulars hypnotized."

"But why would it befriend *her*?"

"Yehti is probably so wracked with grief over Uta, it doesn't know what else to do," said Edgar. "I'll bet it's still bawling its eye out. It's actually kind of wimpy, you know?"

Ellen stared after the trail. "Think we can catch them on foot?"

"No. We need transportation," said Edgar, "and pronto. They got quite a head start."

"Why so glum, twins?" asked Knute, riding up in his golf cart with a golf bag slung over his shoulder. "Your *jennylünd's* not *gåflooten*, is it?"

"Truth be told, Knute," said Ellen, "we're in a bit of a jam. Our, er, friends left without us, and we need to catch up to them or we're going to be in a whole heap of *gåflooten*."

"Say no more, say no more!" said Knute. "Have I got the thing for you. Come on!"

He led the twins down a residential street where many of the homeowners were admiring their new, modern, ice digs. At the end of the lane was a broad shed left largely intact after the explosion. The twins followed Knute inside.

Bëtsye, Knute's specially modified ice dredge, sat within, filling almost the entire shed. Up close, it looked even bigger than the first time the twins had seen it, and they noticed that the front and back were curved like a gondola, and the two rails on which it ran were wide as toboggans.

"Bëtsye here'll get you where you need to go. See, the curvature of the *barnsligs* makes her real aerodynamic. She can reach forty *crickles* an hour!"

"You don't say," said Edgar.

"Yesiree, you'll catch up with your pals in no time," said Knute, patting the dredge.

"You're—you're giving this to us?" asked Ellen.

"Fair trade for finding our bell, I'd say," said Knute, smiling broadly. "I can always make another one. Plenty of material for it, sure. One thing there's gobs of up here is ice!" He winked at the twins.

"Well . . . thank you," Ellen stammered.

"Let's get you set up, then," said Knute, and he went to fetch some reindeer from a nearby pen. In no time two particularly large reindeer were harnessed and strapped to the ice dredge, the sled itself packed with supplies, and the twins and Pet seated atop the driver's bench, Ellen holding the reins.

Knute led the reindeer out to the edge of town, where many of the Frøstenhaveners gathered to see their heroes off.

"Take care!" they shouted. "Stay warm! You'll always have a friend in Frøsthaven! Watch out for *nørbladts*!"

The twins waved good-bye, and Pet saluted.

"Yah!" Ellen cried, and the reindeer took off into the snow, away from the charmingest little town in the Arctic Circle.

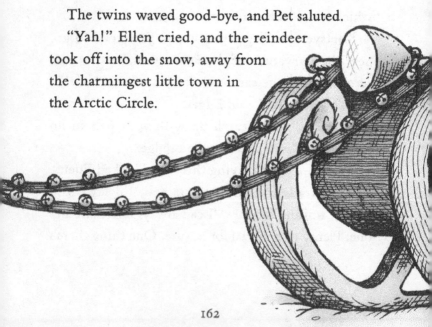

31. The Split

"Whoa!"

Ellen pulled back on the reins, and the two rather rank reindeer came to a halt. She patted one of the beasts with her good hand and hopped down. She stared at the ground and shook her head.

"Bad news, Brother." Ellen kicked a clump of slush up into the air and splattered Edgar. "The snow is melting. Fast."

Edgar dropped the ropes and climbed out of the

sled, the seat of his old pajamas now wet and chilly. "So is our ride, Sister. And the Irregulars are getting harder to track." He knelt and inspected the soggy earth. "Truthfully, after a week of sleigh travel I'm ready for the change. The only problem is, I can't tell what are footprints and what are animal tracks."

"They came this way," said Ellen. "Look." She picked up a pair of gloves they had last seen on Stephanie's hands. "And these look like they could be shoe tracks. And there, white hair." She pulled some strands of white from a bush.

Pet bounced up and down in the snow farther east.

"What is it, Pet?" Edgar approached the hairball and saw that it, too, had found sets of footprints in the melting snow. Two sets looked identical, another was very small, one was long and narrow, and the last was large and pointy.

"There go those cowboy boots again," said Edgar. "The Irregulars must have gone this way."

"And Stephanie and Yehti in the opposite direction," said Ellen. "Maybe they meant to throw us off. They wanted us to find prints leading one way, but they all headed in the other direction."

"But the tracks say otherwise. They really did go in opposite directions. So which way?"

"We follow Stephanie. She's the real danger."

Edgar nodded, but then his eyebrows furrowed.

"What? What's that look for, Edgar?"

"Maybe she wants us to follow her. Maybe she sent the balm with the Irregulars and is trying to lead us after herself." Edgar growled and shook a fist in the air. "Crafty minx!"

Ellen nodded begrudgingly. "And evil as a barbershop quartet."

One of the reindeer snorted and stomped a foot.

"We need to go, Ellen, before we lose the tracks and the daylight. Which way?"

Ellen pointed west. "That way."

"Fine. West it is."

Then she pointed east. "And that way."

"*What?*"

"We need to follow both parties. You know we do."

"But . . . ," said Edgar slowly. "We'd have to split up. You want to split up, Ellen?"

Ellen took the harness off the two reindeer. "It's not a matter of *want*, Edgar."

"I feel really uneasy about this."

Ellen sniffed both reindeer. The smell of the larger beast made her gag. "Here. This one's yours."

"You're serious?"

"Don't be scared, Edgar."

"I'm not *scared*."

"I understand." Ellen hopped onto her reindeer. "It's because I'm older."

"By two minutes!"

Edgar picked up Pet and nervously scratched it. "If we do this, there's a chance we might never—"

"No way," Ellen interrupted. "I don't think I'll get rid of you that easy. The only question now is who Pet should go with."

Edgar took a deep breath and handed Pet up to Ellen. "You'd get lost in a bathtub, Ellen. You'll need Pet's wits more than I will."

Edgar clutched an antler of his reindeer and climbed onto its broad back. "Safe to assume that you'll want to go after—"

"Oh, yes. Stephanie is *mine*."

"I'm after the circus nuts, then."

"Here, you should take these," said Ellen, and she handed over the *Nepenthes* seeds she had pulled from her hand. The twins sat atop their malodorous reindeer for a moment in silence. Ellen finally spoke.

"Let's not make a big deal about this, okay? Ride safe. Find the Irregulars." Her voice choked, but she smiled at her brother. "Don't do anything stupid that causes the complete destruction of the world as we know it."

"We'll go through Miles, right?" asked Edgar. "Both of us communicate through him?"

"And beyond that, we improvise. Come on, it'll be fun."

"Or deadly."

"Same difference."

"Heh." Edgar smirked at his sister. "See you when I see you, then." He tapped the top of his reindeer's head and steered the beast east.

Ellen and Pet watched Edgar's back for a moment as he stole away, and Pet patted Ellen's hand. Then Ellen turned their reindeer toward the pale setting sun, and it clomped westward with the steady thump of earth beneath its heavy hooves. The twins sang along to the beat of the footfalls, until each one's voice faded away into the morning:

> *Just when we thought two can't be beat,*
> *We must split up or face defeat.*
> *I'll take this path, and you, that street,*

Till on the other side we meet.
Good luck, my sibling, on your quest,
As one of us goes east, one west—
I hope you shan't be too depressed
Without me there to tease and jest.
Of course I'll make it on my own,
All by myself . . . just me . . . alone.

Prologue

Two figures wearing striped pajamas tumbled head-
long into a steaming, smoldering pit of red lava at the
bottom of a volcano. Fright and agony were etched
across their faces, but nothing—*nothing*—could save
them now. It was the end of those terrible twins,
Edgar and Ellen.

Stephanie Knightleigh sighed her disappointment
at the lopsided drawing in her notebook. It was
mere fantasy. In reality the twins had escaped the

Black Diamond volcano, each in one piece.

Stephanie flipped through her notebook to pages filled with scribblings, scientific formulas, and other sketches of doomed stick figures. She sat at the counter of the Bandy Station Café, sipping a cranberry phosphate that was far too weak for her liking. Out the window to her left, freight trains moved through the stockyard, and the station hands scurried to and fro, loading cargo. Stephanie tapped her fingers impatiently, then perused more pages, checking off various things and making new notes. She paused on a dense grid of numbers.

"They're all a little different, but the same," she mumbled. "There has to be a sequence that magnifies the power. But things in the woods seem to be going well, according to him." She sneered. "Won't he be surprised."

"Everything to your liking, miss?" The waitress pointed at Stephanie's glass.

"Hardly," Stephanie snapped. "The porter said he'd have my things ready half an hour ago. I'm going to miss my train. Moss grows faster than you people move." She pushed her glass away. "And this phosphate isn't tart enough."

"I'd say you're tart enough as is, dearie." The

waitress snatched up Stephanie's glass and disappeared into the kitchen.

Stephanie huffed and flipped to a page that had a simple list on it:

~~NL~~
~~BD~~
LL
CF
ZZ?
~~QT~~

"Halfway there," she said, and glanced at her watch for the umpteenth time. "What is taking that porter so long?"

Finally a chap in striped overalls entered the café and doffed his cap to Stephanie.

"Miss Knightleigh? She's all packed and ready."

"It's about time," said Stephanie. "Show me."

The porter led Stephanie out through the stockyard, weaving through the rumbling freight trains. They arrived at the very farthest, and the man helped Stephanie into one of the cars. She walked over to a very large crate and inspected it closely, ensuring all the nails and bolts were secure. She plucked a tuft of white hair from an airhole in one of the boards.

"What have you got in there, anyway?" the porter asked. "Sure was heavy. And I think something inside growled at me when we were getting it in here."

"You must be mistaken," Stephanie said coolly. "This is nothing more than a new type of wool . . . heavier than the common variety."

"Good for winter sweaters, I bet," said the porter. He pulled out a clipboard and looked it over. "You're all set. Your package will be delivered to a . . . Smelterburg? Is that right?"

"That is correct," said Stephanie, and she hopped out of the train car. "And now I must be off to *my* next destination," she added as she left the station.

1. A Game of Dice

"That's Pakatchaloosa money," snorted the captain of the *Sea Witch*. "That rot is worthless in New Pakatchaloosa."

Edgar groaned and put the coins back in his satchel. As he rummaged about for another form of payment, he muttered to himself about exchange rates and gold standards and his general bafflement at the workings of the world's currency. He had won a hefty handful of coins in a game of cards with some dodgy-looking crewmen, and while his winnings had bought him passage on the *Sea Witch,* there wasn't enough left over to cover the candy bar he had been caught "borrowing" from the captain's lunch box. None of Edgar's usual schemes to side-step trouble had seemed to work on the savvy crew of the ferry, and now he was cornered.

"Okay, it looks like I don't have any New Pak-atcha-whatever money," said Edgar. "Would you accept a barter for your candy bar? A genuine shark-tooth backscratcher, maybe? Nickel-plated pipe fitting? Mostly uncracked Erlenmeyer flask? Home-made sheriff's badge?"

"Homemade sheriff's badge?" asked the captain, scratching at his eye patch. "What the devil would I do with that?"

"Stop traffic, make arrests, bypass security, con-duct investigations, question suspects—"

"Enough! Eh, I'll take it," said the captain. He snatched the badge. "Now get off my ship and into Grayweather country."

"Grayweather? I thought this was New Palooka," said Edgar.

"When you're a-standing on my boat, you're

in New Pakatchaloosa territory," said the captain, pointing to the purple-and-yellow flag flying from an aft flagpole. "Down at the end of the gangplank is Grayweather Province."

"You're sure this is where those circus performers got off?" asked Edgar.

"Oh, aye," said the captain. "I always keep an eye on circus folk. Especially ones as chipper as that lot. Shifty, they were. Kept my one good eye on 'em till they were off my boat. Don't know where they went after that, and don't care to. 'Tweren't but two days ago, so if you intend to settle a score with them, you best get a move on."

The captain practically shoved Edgar down the gangway.

"Okay, okay, I'm going," said Edgar. "Cripes, I thought that badge meant we were square."

"Even when I get the mustard stains off my steering wheel, the bilge water out of the diesel tanks, and every last pair of boxers untied from the flagpole, we *still* won't be square, you imp," growled the captain. "Take your high-seas mischief and be gone."

Edgar walked down the gangway and took in his surroundings. Grayweather Province was mountainous country: The land beyond the harbor spread out in densely forested foothills and peaks and looked uninhabited. Without further guidance it would be nearly impossible to know which way the Midway Irregulars had gone.

"But I know those circus freaks came this way, and I'm going to catch them," said Edgar. Since parting ways with his sister almost three weeks ago, he had taken to talking to himself. ("I know who'll appreciate hearing my brilliant insights," he had said. "Me!") The reindeer he had ridden out of the Arctic wasteland hadn't seemed to mind his prattling— though one night Edgar's snores grew so loud, they spooked the beast, and it ran off. Edgar had had to follow the trail of the Midway Irregulars on foot, which had been fairly easy until he reached the coast. Fortunately, he had come to a harbor where he met the captain of the *Sea Witch*, who confirmed ferrying the circus kids over to Grayweather.

Now on the far side, Edgar thought to seek out more information on the Midway Irregulars and where they might have gone.

Walking along the harbor, Edgar came upon a group of dockhands playing a game of dice. Edgar felt in his satchel for his own pair of dice, which looked normal to the naked eye but really were fitted with remote-controlled gyroscopes of Edgar's own design.

"Hey, fellas, mind if I rest my feet for a bit and join you?"

The dockhands looked up at the scrawny boy in striped footie pajamas, then at one another. Smiles broke out across all of their sooty faces.

"Why, sure there, lad," said one, who was missing most of his teeth. "Pull up a stool right next to me, here. You ever play dice before?"

"No. Never," said Edgar innocently.

"Even better," said Toothless. The guy next to him, who had a black eye, elbowed him in the ribs.

"What my friend means is, we'll be happy to explain the rules," said Black Eye.

"That's mighty nice of you," said Edgar, and he settled in.

"Sevens and elevens easy up, no loosey deucies, boxcars on top," said Black Eye, rolling the dice.

"You all haven't seen a gaggle of ragtag kids come through here, have you?" Edgar asked as the dice were passed around.

"Yeah, yeah, the *Sea Witch* ferried a crew of nutters like that across the channel a couple days ago," Toothless said. "All smiles and juggling and carrying on, the five of them. What you want them for?"

"They're traveling the world stealing a rare substance that can make a person live forever," Edgar said. "We're not sure what they're doing with it. I suspect they're mixing samples from different locations to make something terrible."

Edgar palmed the dice as they reached him and secretly replaced them with his own gyroscopic dice. He rolled a pair of sixes. "Is that good?"

"Beginner's luck," growled a dockhand whose entire neck was covered in tattoos. Each man handed Edgar a coin.

"Sounds like a pack of right rotten souls you're after, eh?" said Black Eye.

"Not usually," said Edgar. "But at the moment, the Midway Irregulars are under the influence of a hypnotic potion made from the tears of a near-mythical beast."

"You don't say," said Toothless. "Bah," he added as his dice turned up snake eyes.

"I'm carrying some unique seeds that are the antidote to their hypnosis," said Edgar. "The fate of humanity hinges on me catching up to them. Er, so I'm told by my two-hundred-year-old mad-scientist friend."

"Boy, I have heard some whoppers in my day, but this takes all. You hit your head when the ferry docked?" asked Black Eye.

"No, just an overactive imagination, I guess," said Edgar, rolling an eleven. The men all groaned and handed over more coins. "You wouldn't happen to know which way they went, would you?"

Toothless gestured toward shore, where a path wound up into a pine-lined mountain pass. "They went thataway."

"What's up there?" asked Edgar.

The dockhands eyed one another warily.

"Trees," said Black Eye. "Miles and miles of 'em. And wild creatures none too friendly to humans. No one goes into Footwood Forest without a guide. If your circus friends went up there by themselves, likely as not they're dead already."

The men shuddered. Edgar pretended not to notice and picked up the dice, rolling a seven.

"Well, it must just be my lucky day." He chuckled, gathering up everyone's coins. But as he did, Tattoo grabbed his wrist, and the remote button used to control the dice fell out of his sleeve.

"I knew it! Cheat!" shouted Tattoo as the other dockhands jumped to their feet. Edgar backed away from them toward the shore.

"Gee, fellas, it sure has been . . . educational. Great game!" He started to run as Tattoo lunged at him, seizing him by the collar. Edgar threw all his purloined coins onto the dock and, in the men's haste to retrieve them, managed to struggle free. He bolted for the forest, zigzagging up the steep path until he had disappeared amid the bracken.

Back on the docks, the men had gathered up their money and stood looking after the fleeing boy. None moved to follow him.

"He'll get his," said Black Eye. "He'll be lost before dusk, and that's when the Squatch will get 'im."

Read where the

BOOK 1

Edgar & Ellen: Rare Beasts

Edgar and Ellen dream BIG when it comes to pranks. After they learn that exotic animals are worth tons of money, the twins devise a get-rich-quick scheme that sends Nod's Limbs into a frenzy!

BOOK 2

Edgar & Ellen: Tourist Trap

Mayor Knightleigh wants to turn little Nod's Limbs into a premiere vacation destination. But Edgar and Ellen have a plan to give the too-sweet townspeople all the attention they deserve!

BOOK 3

Edgar & Ellen: Under Town

Someone is causing a lot of trouble in town, but it isn't Edgar and Ellen! To catch this new mischievous miscreant, the twins must scour the sewers and uncover someone's dirty secret.